Despite myself, I began to respond. I knew what she was doing. I've done it plenty of times myself. Sex as Novocain.

She tugged off my suit jacket, pressed me against the desk, her mouth migrating to my earlobe, sucking, pleading. "Make me forget, baby, please, for a little while. Take me out of my head." Her hands yanked up my shirttails, ran along my back and plucked the hooks of my bra. Moist palms traced the line of my torso, clutched my waist as she lowered her head and pulled greedily on my nipples. Her flame caught me. I groaned out loud, feeling my body clutch, desperate for fingers, tongue. I opened my shirt, then hers and we rocked against each other, knees interlocked, an erotic battle for dominance. She undid my zipper, rubbed me through my underpants until the ache became unbearable. I flipped us around, backed her onto the desk and lifted her ankle-length skirt up around her hips. She was already naked underneath. I chuckled to myself. These religious women are something else.

About the Author

Jaye Maiman has written four previous romantic mysteries featuring the private investigator Robin Miller: *I Left My Heart,* the Lambda Literary Award winner *Crazy for Loving, Under My Skin,* and Lambda Literary Award nominee *Someone to Watch.* Born in Brooklyn, New York, Jaye Maiman grew up in a Coney Island housing project where she spent Tuesday nights consuming blueberry cheese knishes and watching fireworks from a beachside boardwalk. She resides in Brooklyn with her two puppy cats and her partner, playmate, editor, co-neurotic and magic-maker Rhea.

The 5th Robin Miller Mystery

JAYE MAIMAN

THE NAIAD PRESS, INC.
1996

Printed in the United States of America on acid-free paper
First Edition

Editor: Christine Cassidy
Cover designer: Bonnie Liss (Phoenix Graphics)
Typesetter: Sandi Stancil

Library of Congress Cataloging-in-Publication Data

Maiman, Jaye, 1957–
  Baby, it's cold / by Jaye Maiman.
     p.   cm.
  ISBN 1-56280-141-4 HB   ISBN 1-56280-156-2 PB
  1. Miller, Robin (Fictitious character) — Fiction.
I. Title.
PS3563.A38266B3   1996
813'.54—dc20   96-8544
                                                                  CIP

Dedicated to the memory of my aunt,
Lila Roseman,
and in honor and respect for my uncle,
Ed Roseman,
whose unquenched thirst for life reminds
me to drink deep.

Acknowledgments

Braving a blank computer screen is no easy task — especially the way that blinking cursor shouts, *"Feed me, momma!"* while the hard drive hums like a sadistic psychiatrist: *"Mmm, interesting. Still no ideas."* What gives me the courage to tackle the keyboard over and over is the support and encouragement I receive from my fans, my dearest friends, and my incredible partner in life, love and angst. Rhea, you continue to astound me. I *leetz* you. So there.

Special thanks to —

Jill, for giving me the first thumb's up . . .
Carmela, for her support and proofreading expertise . . .
Shalom, for another round of insightful questions and gentle suggestions . . .
Gary, for being the best brother-in-law a lesbian could ever have . . .

And always to my Mom and Dad (if only the world had a heart as big as yours), and the gaggle of friends who make my life so wonderful . . . Pauline, Risa, Elaine, Annie, Joan, Jill, Mark, Scott, Maureen, Victoria, and the Hamlet den mother and father, Dale and Roy.

Chapter 1

Most of the time I think of change as a gradual thing, an evolution that outsiders can witness if they're sharp enough, like the way the sky clouds over and unfurls fists of rain on a day that started out so blue and clean it made waking up seem like a dream. But sometimes change is quick. By the time you get around to noticing it, the process is done. *Finis.*

You know those magic capsules they make for kids? You drop one into a glass of water and one blink later you're staring at some foam-green sea monster. Well, sometimes change is that fast. Once the momentum's on, you can't stop it, can't jump out of the way, can't even predict where it's rushing you to. You're flat on your back on the biggest goddamn wave and just praying you can keep your mouth shut until you hit land.

The wave picked me up at ten after one, Monday afternoon. I was in a meeting with my partner, Tony. The two of us run the Serra Investigative Agency. If a less likely pair exists, drop me a postcard. About the only thing we have in common is our love of strong coffee and rich food. Tony's an ex-cop with a penchant for quoting the Bible and sucking up to rich folk. Rich folk make me break out in hives. The odd part is, I'm rich. I used to be Laurel Carter, an author of highly florid and highly profitable romance novels with titles like *Love's Lost Flame* and *The Blazing Heart*. Embarrassing stuff, but the royalties keep me flush in Twinkies and Yoo-Hoos so I don't complain.

Further complicating matters between me and my partner is the fact that I'm a lesbian and he's a recovering bigot who contracted HIV from a blood transfusion many moons ago. The kicker is we've grown to like each other.

Right then, Tony and I were arguing about a disgruntled client we had met at a neighborhood restaurant an hour before. The woman's coat never even made it to the spare chair. She undid the top button of her coat, stabbed a finger at the new lesion on Tony's neck, muttered something inane like, "I knew about her, but *you*? My God!" Then she pivoted on her elegant pencil-thin heels and clacked away. My attitude was *screw her*, but the lady had pumped a few grand into our modest business and had fully intended to spill several more, and Tony hated the idea of all that sweet green seeping into someone else's back pocket.

The phone rang and I snapped it up. "SIA. Miller speaking."

Tony and I stared at each other over my desk, hard and mean looks, like bulldogs facing off over a feverish bitch. The truth is I'd rather fight for seven days straight than face the facts. Death was sniffing at Tony's heels, licking its greedy chops. And this was one fierce dog neither of us could beat back.

A familiar, inarticulate squeal on the other end of the phone announced the caller. I said, "Hey Bethala, is that my munchkin I hear?"

"Carol's fine, just fine," she said, answering a question I hadn't asked. My eyebrows arched.

Beth, Dinah and I are housemates in Park Slope, Brooklyn — Mecca for lesbians and anachronistic progressives. Beth's a nurse who works mornings at Methodist Hospital. Her partner's a therapist who works out of the brownstone we jointly own. Carol's their adopted daughter. Tony leaned forward suddenly and asked, "What's wrong?" I waved him off and repeated his question to Beth.

"A baby's missing from the drop-off center," she said.

"Missing?" My brain immediately retrieved a *Daily News* headline from two months earlier: "Missing Baby Assumed Dead!"

She hesitated. "It's Michael."

I closed my eyes tight and rubbed my hand over my face. "Fuck. Does Phyl know?"

"Yeah. She just got here. She's pretty stunned. She's refusing to call the police. You know . . . "

I sure as hell did. Back in September, a baby had been kidnapped from a nearby Brooklyn day-care center. The feds pounced, the media snapped into sympathetic hysteria, and the parents kept every dime of the $100,000 ransom money. Only problem, the baby and the kidnapper were never found. The feds chased their tails until they tied the case into one impenetrable knot. There had been no more threatening phone calls since early October. No more heartbreaking tapes of the baby's cries. Just utter, devastating silence.

I said, "I'll be right there," then hung up and quickly updated Tony. We never work a case together, but when he grabbed his coat this time I didn't argue. Given my personal stake in the case, Tony's presence would be welcome.

Phyllis and I have been dating for about eight weeks now. As Tony locked the office door, I remembered the way Michael had tried to swallow my nose when I put him to bed last night. I raced outside, Tony breathing hard behind me. My only thought was, damn Beth for setting me up with Phyllis. I should have listened to my instincts when I had the chance. Blind dates are today's equivalent of the ancient Roman arena where gladiators engaged in mortal combat for the amusement of the untouched masses. The best way to survive the battle is to avoid getting trapped in the first place. Unfortunately, Beth had caught me when my shields were down.

We'd been skidding into *the* holiday season, ho-ho-ho, popping Champagne corks and all that heartbreaking merriment. My standard MO for coping was duck and cover. But Beth had other plans.

I dropped my jaw and said, "You want to set me up with a nouveau lesbo with an eleven-month-old son? Honey, motherhood's done something frightening to your mind."

"That's unfair."

"What's unfair is expecting me to be interested in a woman who married her college sweetheart, spent a good nine years playing happy homemaker before dropping her bundle of joy, and then woke up one morning with a sinus headache and a hankering for women in uniform. Come on, Beth. She's been with just one woman. For all you know, that affair with the Philly cop was just a nasty blip on her heterosexual radar."

"It wasn't a blip. She was crazy about Linda. Besides, these feelings aren't new to her. Phyllis and Matthew married precisely because they knew they both had homosexual tendencies. They were scared, Robin, that's all. It happens all the time. I give them credit for not wasting the rest of their lives play-acting."

"Fine. Sign them up for *Oprah,* but I'm not interested. Jeez. She'd probably bore me to death with tales of diaper laundering and colicky nights. Give her a copy of *Our Bodies, Our Selves,* but leave me out of it."

"She's not an idiot, Rob. She's socially conscious, volunteers at the crisis center on Ninth Street. Freelances as a real estate agent. The woman's attractive *and* she has a brain. What else do you want?"

"How about no son? I'm not ready to be a step-mom."

"God, you're impossible. First of all, Phyllis isn't interested in anything long-term. She and Matthew divorced over a year ago, amicably I might add, and she just wants to have some fun. Second, the holidays are coming, and she doesn't want to be alone any more than you do . . ."

"I won't be alone. I'll be with you guys."

Her pink lips went white.

Enunciating carefully, I said, "I *will* be with you, won't I?"

Beth lifted Carol from her lap and placed her in the soft-sided playpen. Our eyes never met. "Well," she said quietly. "This year we decided to visit my parents in Chicago. They haven't seen Carol in six months . . ."

"You're leaving me?" I asked. I couldn't remember the last time the three of us hadn't spent the holidays together.

"My dad's not well, Robin."

I felt small, petty and mighty peeved. Okay, so the man has Alzheimer's. But what about me? A stupid move over the summer had destroyed the most promising relationship I had ever known, and I was feeling pretty damn pathetic.

Do you know what it's like to lose a woman as amazing as K.T. Bellflower? Imagine a ship bound for glorious Hawaii that's seized by an unexpected storm and battered by the Pacific surf until nothing's left but a single, gnarled piece of driftwood. And not the picturesque kind, either, but the kind that's coated with grimy seaweed and studded with tar and barnacles. The interior is rotted and the outside's as pale as bone. Now, picture me. I was in worse shape. It was the kind of breakup where people I hardly knew felt compelled to search me out just to tell me what an asshole I'd been. As a result, I was feeling a wee bit needy and a little less than charitable. Never underestimate the power of loneliness to reduce a person to their basest instincts.

I rapidly scanned my mental data bank of alternatives. My friends Amy and Carly had already planned a vacation in Puerto Rico. My sister and brother traditionally spend the holidays with my mother in Florida, where I am the perpetual *persona non grata*. My partner, Tony, visits his sister. The conclusion was startling: without my housemates, I'd be alone. Alone during the holidays. Things could be worse, of course. I pictured myself slumped in the shadow of the Old Glory they left planted in the moon's cold, thin crust, while back on distant Earth universal peace and harmony erupted and scientists announced that hot fudge could accelerate weight loss.

I asked, "Should I slash my wrists now, or is it better to wait until Dinah gets home?"

Beth smiled and shook her head indulgently. "So, do you want to meet Phyllis?"

The blind date suddenly sounded appealing. I took

a deep breath. "Okay, does she have buck teeth, or what?"

I found out for myself just three nights later.

No buck teeth. No siree.

For some reason, probably because she had spent the last decade as a straight married woman and the last year as a breast-feeding slave to a mini-man, I assumed Phyllis would be matronly. I rang the doorbell reluctantly, fully expecting it to be opened by a dumpy, thick-waisted lady in a house dress and pink fuzzy slippers. And, of course, she'd have the requisite cheesy diaper draped over her shoulder. Boy, was I wrong.

It was a cold day in December. I wore an Eddie Bauer sweater, turtleneck, corduroy pants and thermal socks. Phyllis, on the other hand, wore a hunter green silk shell, no bra. A strand of tiny, luminescent pearls teased her cleavage. Her skirt was short and black and wrapped tightly around her hips. It may have been my imagination, but I would have sworn that she was emitting mini A-bombs of musk.

After a moment, I forced my eyes back to her face. The smile I found there told me my reaction had not gone unnoticed. Even her posture said, *take your time.* I continued my scrutiny. She had almond eyes that looked almost Oriental, a nice pouty mouth, high cheeks, a boyish haircut and a Katherine Hepburn chin. She did not look like a mother.

She reached out a long-fingered hand with recently clipped and clearly buffed nails and pulled me inside. There were no Tonka toys in sight. No crib. No unsightly diapers. The only evidence of a baby was the hint of talcum powder in the air.

"You're a brave woman," she said to my back.

Then she clasped onto the collar of my jacket and confidently tugged it down my arms.

I'd been single and suffering but by no means celibate since I broke up with K.T. in July. I enjoyed a convenient, emotionless arrangement with a performer who lives in Provincetown. The woman was very willing and able to scratch my occasional itch. Nevertheless, my hairs stood on end as Phyllis's fingers lightly brushed my arms. There's nothing like being undressed by a woman who means business. When she stopped at the jacket, I sighed.

She straightened the back of my turtleneck. "Do you realize that in the past year I haven't had a single date? Not one. I've been to the bars, tried the personal ads, everything. You lesbians are a hard bunch."

I flinched at the "you lesbians" and turned around. She had crossed the room and was hanging my jacket in the front closet. It was clear she had no intention to take this date out on the town. She closed the door, smoothed her skirt down over her attractive full butt and faced me. I had to disagree. Us lesbians weren't a hard bunch. Not at all.

"I can't imagine you going unnoticed at a bar."

"I didn't say unnoticed. They noticed all right. But apparently no one was interested in an observant, recent divorcée with an infant son."

A faint alarm sounded. "Observant?"

She cocked her head, then said, "I see Beth omitted some details when she described me."

"Details?" I repeated. I wanted to run for the phone.

"I come from a religious family . . . and I still keep a Kosher home. Is that a problem?"

Oh, Beth, I thought, you sure do have a queer sense of humor. My father was a holocaust survivor who viewed his Jewish heritage as a form of leprosy. Only at my mother's insistence had we observed the major holidays at all, and always quietly, behind locked doors and heavily curtained windows. I asked, "Do you travel on the Sabbath?" in what sounded to my ears like a mousy squeal.

She shook her head in the negative. I was about to make a beeline for the door when she made a beeline for me. She came within six inches of me. Damn it if she didn't smell good. Now, I hate when that happens. My mind said, *run*, but my body said, *hold on, kid, let's see where this bronco wants to roam.*

Phyllis bit her bottom lip, took hold of my belt loops, then said, "Let me put it this way. I've made love with a woman exactly six times. Almost eighteen months ago. Before that, my husband and I went three years without sex. My favorite vibrator went on the fritz nine weeks ago, and you're the first single lesbian I've had in my home since that tragic event. More to the point, I'm HIV negative, hungry, willing and interested in nothing more than the next twelve hours. You can walk out now, or . . ."

I think she kissed me first. Not that it matters. The important part is that she wasn't lying. Her mouth was greedy, her body a live wire. When I stroked her back, the moan she emitted was downright primal and one of the sexiest sounds I'd ever heard. I could have broken off the embrace, but by then I was convinced that I had a public service to perform.

She came so fast the first time I barely had time

to blink. Things slowed down after that. We had sex on the coffee table, the staircase, and finally her bed. It wasn't until nine the next morning that I remembered she had a kid.

We both heard the downstairs door at the same time. I propped myself up on one elbow, immediately alert. Phyllis jerked out of bed, grabbed a robe and scampered downstairs. No words were exchanged. I was naked and had to remain that way. The only item of clothing that had made it to the bedroom were my socks. I put those on and opened the door a crack.

I heard a man laugh. "Well, congrats, hon. Do you want me to keep Michael the rest of the weekend?"

Phyllis was quick to answer. "No way, Matt. My family's coming by later. Michael has to be here."

They said their good-byes quickly. The next thing I knew she was back upstairs, her son cradled in her arms. I hate to admit it, but it was like finding a snake in the garden. The bedroom suddenly seemed unsafe.

We stared at each other over his body. Phyl was no slouch in the mind-reading department. "You want your clothes?" she asked.

I nodded. She thrust Michael into my arms and left the room. The kid was unbelievably heavy and dense, like a sack of cat litter. Since I was still naked, I felt weird holding him against my body. I stood there, arms outstretched, feeling vaguely obscene and distinctly uncomfortable. Finally, my muscles gave in and I placed him on the bed. His eyelids flickered open as I tucked the blanket around his waist. He wiggled his little eyebrows, shot me a killer smile and it was all over. Phyllis was history. I had fallen in love.

Second Home, the drop-off center in which Michael should be safely ensconced, was on Lincoln Place between Fourth and Fifth avenues, about a fifteen-minute walk from my office. We made it in eight. We rounded the last corner like twin running backs. I sideswiped a mailman and Tony overturned his cart. He muttered, "Sorry," but marched on like Patton leading a brigade into battle. I gritted my teeth and bent to help scoop up the letters and magazines papering the damp concrete. You wouldn't believe how many people order *Playboy* and *TV Guide*. I gathered an armload, then righted the cart. The mailman stood by all the time. As I dumped my load into one of two twin cotton sacks, each large enough to carry a week's laundry, he used a corner of someone's *Reader's Digest* to pick between his teeth. I decided, screw the nice routine, and said, "The rest is yours."

He scratched his ear and glared at me over his eagle beak of a nose. "Sure. Leave the civil servant to clean up the mess. Ain't that the way?"

My internal hard drive clicked off all the recent incidents in which postal workers had snapped into wholesale violence. I scampered past eagle-nose and caught up with Tony.

Beth and Phyllis were sitting on the stoop, each of them clasping mugs from which steam rose. Phyl glanced up, saw me and shuddered so forcefully coffee sloshed over the mug's lip and splashed over her lap. She didn't even flinch.

I went to Beth first, hugged her, then said, "Why aren't you both inside? It's freezing out here."

Phyllis answered. "It's my fault. I can't stand to be . . ." Her voice cracked. I sat next to her.

Tony nodded at both women, lifted his wool collar to cover the lesion no coat could cover, then coughed into his hand. "I'm going inside."

When he was gone, Phyl said, "I don't want him involved."

I didn't like her tone. "Tony's a good man. And a great detective."

"He's an ex-cop. I don't want cops involved. I don't want some macho asshole building a career on my son's life. Beth understands, don't you?" She took hold of Beth's ankle. "You'd feel the same way if it was Carol . . . I know it. Maybe Robin just doesn't get it." Her eyes were bloodshot and swollen, her skin mottled and lips blue-tinged.

The mailman rolled toward us through the hip-high gate. He threw Phyllis and Beth a wide smile and slipped me a curled lip. I grabbed the wad of envelopes and magazines from him with a cursory nod. He started to protest, then thought better of it. I wasn't in the mood for negotiation. He retreated to the other side of the gate, then made a big show of sorting through the next mail drop, tsking with exaggerated concern. The guy acted like I had personally brought down the U.S. postal system. I turned back to Phyl and lowered my voice. "Let's talk about this inside. The last thing we need is for you to get sick." I raised her by the elbow and opened the front door. Beth took the mug from Phyl's hands and led the way.

As Phyl walked by me, I asked her if she had called her husband yet. She muttered something about a busy signal, then followed Beth down the hallway. I peeked into the waiting area in the front room and decided that that's where I belonged.

I found Tony perched on a wood chair salvaged from a defunct public school. He looked oddly comfortable. The man once topped two hundred pounds and boasted the thick no-neck physique of a former football player. But sitting there, his slim butt propped on a delicate slab of maple, his two-sizes-too-large overcoat billowing up from his shoulders, he resembled an adolescent boy who had not yet grown into his body. I shifted my attention to the woman sitting ramrod straight in the armchair opposite him.

I sometimes pick Carol up when my housemates can't, so I recognized the woman at once. Karen Alexander was a queen-sized blonde, five-foot-eight, maybe one-ninety on days she retained water. A good-looking woman, more handsome than pretty, the kind you'd trust to bandage a knee, tend your garden or haul your child over the Himalayas. Her hands were square and broad, her nails short. I took in the brushed gold wedding band, the too-delicate herring-bone bracelet, then locked onto her denim-blue eyes. Her expression was impenetrable.

Tony glanced up at me. "Ms. Alexander runs this place."

I said, "I know," and extended my hand. Karen's grasp was solid, her palm sweaty.

"I'm surprised to see *both* of you," she said

hastily. "Phyl specifically asked me to keep this low-profile."

"And you agree with that approach?" I asked.

Karen averted her eyes. "No one wants a repeat of the Alice Breen incident." She was referring to the recent kidnapping. "The next parent's due here in about an hour. If she sees *him*," she said, jabbing her chin at Tony, "she'll panic. No insult meant, but everything about you screams cop."

Tony smiled. "No insult at all. Matter of fact, I take that as the highest compliment, 'specially if you mean I stink like a New York cop. Now, if you're so hot to get me out of here, I suggest you stop worrying about covering your ass and get down to business."

Karen stiffened. "My business, Mr. Serra, is taking care of the babies in the back room."

Tony sniffed. "Then I gotta say, you're not so good at your business, are you?"

Her mouth twitched. She stood abruptly and crossed to the windows. With her fingers hooked between the slats of a mahogany shutter, she said, "No one can talk to me like that, not you, not anyone." Her voice was low and tremulous. I felt more surprised than sympathetic. The first time I had met Beth at the center I witnessed a gaggle of infants attacking Karen Ninja-style, and the stoic administrator had not even blinked.

Now she turned to leave the room. I blocked her path. "Karen, no one's questioning your abilities. You have to remember, this is about Michael," I said softly. "My partner's just anxious —"

Tony interrupted. "While you're soft-pedaling me

to this lady, Miller, the kidnapper's cruising away at a steady seventy. In cases like this, a good cop doesn't give a shit about egos. A kid's life's at stake. We've got twenty-four hours tops before that boy's ready for the dust fields. Every goddamn second steals a decade from that kid's life. So if the two of you are done chatting ..."

Karen's gaze shifted from me to Tony and then back again. After a moment she sat down and said, "I'm not thinking clearly right now. Micky's always been special to me."

Tony jumped. "Micky? Do his parents call him Micky?" His question sounded accusatory, even to my ears.

Karen glared at him, her lips tight.

Tony was way off his game. My partner never grills suspects; his usual questioning style is sympathetic and seamlessly manipulative. I've seen nimble-footed corporate lawyers stumble confidently over Tony's verbal tripwires. But if he persisted in challenging Karen this way, she'd clam up so tight we'd need a crowbar to pry out the smallest grain of fact.

I tapped Tony on the shoulder. "Why don't you go talk with Phyllis?"

His head snapped in my direction. The message in his eyes was clear: *don't dismiss me.*

I gently added, "Phyl knows you, Tony. Maybe you can convince her we need to contact the authorities. Please. She won't listen to me."

"Sure, Miller," he said, then he leaned over and planted his still-beefy hands on both arms of the chair in which Karen sat. "You know the biggest mistake rookie cops make? They overlook the obvious.

Too much television, I guess. My lou once told me, "Tony, you enter a crime scene, first thing you do is check the faces around you. Nine times out of ten, you're staring right into the perp's eyes.'" He straightened up. "If you've got something to hide, lady, I'm gonna find it. And if I find it after the kid's dead, I promise you, you'll pay in ways you can't even begin to imagine." To me, he said, " 'Whoever commits sin is the servant of sin.' John eight, thirty-four."

He swaggered out. Tony Serra as Clint Eastwood. Or maybe Jerry Falwell. Before disappearing into the hallway he paused dramatically to examine the center's permit, then turned, made a gun barrel from his thumb and index finger and shot Karen with a little cluck of his tongue.

Karen was not amused. "What a pig. How do you stand him?"

Unintentionally or not, Tony had paved the way for me to ride in on the proverbial white steed. I saddled up and said, "I need his contacts, that's about it. I can't tell you how sorry I am for the way he spoke to you. You must be going through hell."

She stood up and strode toward me, a distinct limp in no way slowing her progress. "Men like him are probably what makes lesbianism seem so attractive to women like you," she said, as if she had uncovered the Rosetta Stone.

Actually, it's women like Melissa Etheridge and k.d. lang that make lesbianism so attractive, but I bit my tongue and said instead, "Why don't we sit down and start from the beginning."

I watched her sink into a Queen Anne chair donated by a local family. "Nothing unusual happened today, well, except for, you know ..." As she spoke, she massaged her right hip unconsciously, as if by long habit. She looked close to tears. "I always put the children to nap at eleven-forty-five. Promptly. My ritual is very effective. Any noise disturbs them, so I turn on the sound machine and the color wheel —"

I stopped her and asked for an explanation.

"Oh, the color wheel's just a lamp that uses a rotating panel of gels to project colors onto the ceiling. I use it myself sometimes when I'm particularly restless. The effect is somewhat hypnotizing. Within minutes, the children are dead asleep, I mean —"

"I know what you mean. What happened next?"

"I sent Livy out, you know, my assistant." I nodded. "Well, she left and then the phone rang. I picked up in the kitchen, since there's no phone in the middle room where the babies sleep. I was on the phone for no more than a few minutes —"

"Who was it?"

"Who?" She hesitated, then said, "My husband," but I didn't like the way she looked. Like a kid hiding a bad report card.

"Can I have his name and a number where I can reach him?"

Her expression darkened. "He's out of town. On the road. That's why I had to take the call."

I made a note to check her story, then asked her to continue.

"Tripp, my husband, put me on hold. While I was waiting, I put up water for tea ... I take my lunch while the children are napping. By the time he got back on, the tea was ready. I sat down with the paper, right here." She massaged the table top. The

New York Times was folded open to the food section. "Around twelve-forty, I heard a little cry come over the room monitor over there, near the fridge, so I went in to check." She covered her eyes, a gesture that could have been guilt, sorrow or deceit. "Micky was gone."

"You heard nothing suspicious over the room monitor?"

"No. Just the usual ruffling of bed sheets and —"

Phyl's voice roared toward us from the back of the apartment. "I don't know, I don't know," she shouted repeatedly. A chorus of wails erupted at once from the speaker at Karen's elbow. She sprang from her chair, spat the words, "Goddamn it," and ran through the hallway into the kitchen. I was on her heel. Over Karen's shoulder I saw Tony and Phyl facing off outside the middle room where the babies had been sleeping.

Beth opened the door with a red-faced baby in her arms. Carol's mouth quivered as she howled. "This is insane," Beth sputtered.

Karen pressed Beth back into the room, then snapped the door shut behind her. Phyl and Tony glared at me. I said, "What?" and they both started talking at the same time.

"Why'd you bring this asshole?" Phyl demanded, while Tony said, "I'm outta here," and stormed past me. Meanwhile, I could just make out the hum of a lullaby being sung by Karen and Beth in the other room.

"You don't give a shit about Michael," Phyl snarled at me before bursting into tears. I folded her into my arms and waited until she stopped trembling. Suddenly, she pushed me away, wiped her nose with

19

the back of her hand and said, "You don't understand. You can't. You've never had a kid."

Maybe she was right. I stood there remembering the time a friend inadvertently allowed one of my cats to escape out the front door. I scoured the neighborhood for three hours before I found poor Mallomar shivering between two garbage cans on the next block. But I didn't let myself cry until that little scum-coated, furry body was back in my arms. It was an unfair comparison, I know, but I felt impatient with Phyllis for wasting time.

With effort, I asked, "What do you want me to do, Phyl?"

She stared at me dumbly. "Nothing. Just stay with me until we get him back."

Oh boy. I pretended to clean the corner of one eye. "How do you expect to get him back?"

The peal of a phone startled us both. Phyl barreled past me and snapped up the receiver.

"Yes," she said breathlessly. "That's me."

I pressed my ear on the other side of the phone. The voice sounded almost computerized, but the message was clear. "Forty-eight hours . . . two hundred and fifty thousand dollars, in unmarked C-notes, random serial numbers. Your fancy-ass dad should be able to arrange that. There are three white laundry bags in the hallway bench. Use them. Wait for further instructions. Any police involvement, the boy's dead. I swear, I'll slit his throat and feed him to the rats. And, Phyl, the jackass who just left there better not show his fucking face again or I'll make the kill real slow and nasty."

The kidnapper had seen Tony.

I barreled toward the front of the brownstone. The door slammed shut behind me just as the squeal of tires reverberated from Fourth Avenue. I didn't bother running. The tidal wave had begun.

Chapter 2

"Phyl, I'm not an expert in this type of crime. It goes beyond me, beyond the cops. The feds —"

"We've settled this. I'll get the money from my parents. Michael's their life. They won't squawk over the ransom." She leaned over and whispered harshly in my ear. "I swear to God, Robin, if you put Michael's life in jeopardy, I'll have your license pulled. I'm not joking."

Phyllis, Karen and I were sitting around the kitchen table. Beth had not left Carol's side. She remained in the middle room. I could hear her on the other side of the door cooing insipid Disney songs among the babies as if all were right with the world.

I stared at Phyllis with surprise. She knew enough of my predilections as a private eye, including my fondness for breaking and entering, to get me in plenty of hot water. My first reaction was to get up and storm out, indignant and indifferent. Then I realized Phyl was in high-mother mode. In the animal kingdom, no one messes with momma. I spoke softly. "Phyl, calling in the feds may be the only way to get Michael home safely. The Breen case isn't typical —"

"I'm siding with Phyllis on this," Karen said stiffly. "Maybe you live in a different world, but neither the police nor the FBI have given me cause to believe in their competence. The kidnappers want money. And excuse me, Phyllis, but the Roths certainly have money. So why not pay them? Do you remember what happened when the Breen baby disappeared? I do. The parents called in the FBI and all hell broke loose. Everyone had their own agenda. Catch the bad guys. Keep the hundred grand. Sell more papers. It was a zoo."

"And what happens when the money's paid, huh? You really think these monsters will just hand Michael over?" I asked.

Phyl straightened up. "Yes. If they get what they want. Yes."

Karen interjected, "Won't the money be marked anyway? I mean, they have to have a way to trace the cash."

"Christ. Why are we talking about money? The point is *Michael*, getting him home safely."

Karen slapped her palms against the table.

23

"Enough. This is Phyllis's decision. Go ahead, Phyl, and call your parents."

I felt my teeth chomp together. These idiots were going to get Michael killed. I stood up and latched onto Phyllis's wrist as she dialed her parents. "Listen, what about Matthew? Doesn't he get a vote on this?" I was playing dirty pool. I hadn't met Phyl's ex-husband, but I knew he adored his son.

Phyl pulled her hand away. "Matthew's used to my taking control. I've done it for nearly a decade."

"At the very least, let me look into this. It's not about the money. If you want to pay off the kidnappers, fine. Frankly, I don't give a shit. All I care about is Michael's safety. Okay?"

She turned her back to me and spoke into the phone, "Hello, Mother."

"Phyl?"

She cupped a palm over the mouthpiece and glanced at me. "You'll be discreet. No scare tactics. And no Tony."

She wasn't asking questions. She was issuing orders. I took them like a champ.

I left her and headed into the middle room. Karen's assistant, Olivia Walker, had returned from lunch shortly before we arrived. She was around twenty-one and wore her hair shoe-polish black and seriously spiked. The ring piercing her nose was gold and the one through her eyebrow silver. Her leather jacket boasted mega studs, ripped elbows and a button depicting Ursula, the octopus witch from Disney's *The Little Mermaid*. She was the picture of wholesome punk, clear-eyed and adorable, with a Julie Andrews voice. It was the mild Cockney lilt that convinced most parents she could be trusted

24

alone in a room full of infants ranging from six to twenty-four months. She was a gentle soul who listened to rock bands with names like Ax Murderers or Road Kill. But when she sang "Itsy, Bitsy Spider," there wasn't a baby around who didn't stare up at her as if she were heaven and earth, breast and bottle combined.

Beth looked toward me as she changed a little boy's diaper. She shouldn't have turned her head. A stream of pale urine shot her in the chin. "Oh damn," she said without rancor.

Meanwhile Olivia bobbed around the room with a baby the size of an overstuffed knapsack. The kid's head was coated with hair the color of overripe cantaloupe. "Can't believe this," she muttered. "It's 'orrible, that's what it is, just 'orrible. When Beth told me, I nearly lost my lunch. Poor Mick."

Beth broke off a sob, lifted the boy she was changing and moved over to an empty crib on the far side of the room.

I turned to Olivia. "Where were you when this happened?"

She nodded at a second door that led back into the hallway. "Mind if we step outside for a bit?" she asked, not waiting for a reply. The cigarette was already in her hand. Neither of us stopped to retrieve a jacket but, unlike me, Olivia didn't seem to notice the frigid temperature. I hugged myself for warmth and waited for her to start.

"The mistress Karen — she's tickled by that nickname, Mistress Karen, says it makes her feel rather baroque — she's strict about the babies' nap time, she is. Quarter of twelve, the babies go down. Fifteen after the hour, I break for lunch."

"Did you see anything unusual when you left?"

She laughed, the smoke curling past her sparkling eyes. "It's Park Slope, love. When don't I see something a bit odd? Mum thinks that's why I moved here. Could be she's right. There's a bloke who walks by every afternoon with a boa constrictor wrapped 'round his neck like a bloody scarf. Last week a woman relieved herself in a kitty box right outside the door, she just squatted down and did her business. Gawd."

"No one was parked outside? Or standing nearby?"

She squinted, sucked hard on the cigarette. "No . . . well, maybe."

My toes were going numb. I stamped my feet.

"There was —" Olivia's attention shifted to a spot over my shoulder. "Good afternoon, Mrs. DeVine," she said suddenly.

I looked behind me. A woman wisely garbed in a canary yellow Land's End parka walked toward us at a brisk pace. "Sorry I'm late. Is Sophie ready?"

Olivia and I shared quick uneasy looks. She recovered first. With a surprisingly natural laugh, she said, " 'Fraid she had herself one awesome poop this morning, but she should be spanking clean by now. Beth Morris stopped by earlier to drop off Carol. She's still inside, helping the mistress. I'll join you in a few."

The woman hurried by me without a glance, inserted a key into the door and let herself in.

Olivia said, "I better go back. We take in eight babies over two shifts. Mrs. DeVine's the first afternoon pick-up."

My gaze hadn't shifted from the door. "DeVine has a key?"

"Sure. So does your friend Beth. All the parents are given outside keys so they feel more at home. The personal touch, we call it. Truth be told, this way we don't have to listen to the bloody buzzer all day."

My temple pulsed wildly. Eight babies. Eight families. All with keys to the center. And two days to find Michael. "What kind of files do you keep on the families who bring their kids here?" I asked. My facial skin felt tight. I had a strange impulse to start running, but I didn't know where.

Olivia nailed the cigarette under her boot heel. "You'd have to ask Karen."

As if on cue, the door opened. Karen said, "Enough talk. The babies must be picking up on something because they're bringing down the walls. I need you inside now."

Olivia rolled her eyes at me, then sashayed after Karen. I followed. We collided into Mrs. DeVine and her baby lump in the hallway. I pressed myself against the wall to let them pass, then without a word, I retraced my steps. Karen didn't try to stop me.

"Uh, Mrs. DeVine?" The woman had already trotted down the stoop. She stopped and turned, shifting the cantaloupe-head baby I had noticed earlier deeper into a sling that hung underneath the parka. I extended my hand. "I'm with the Bureau of Day Care, Bedford district. I'd offer you a business card, but they're in my coat pocket." I gestured at my meager navy wool crepe suit, an outfit selected for the sake of the uppity client who had stiffed me and my partner earlier in the day.

Mrs. DeVine gave me a good once-over, lifted a hood over Sophie's blinding tresses, then jutted her chin toward the building. "Has Second Home been cited for some type of violation?"

"Absolutely not. This is routine. Do you have a few minutes?"

"Not really. Sophie weighs a solid thirty-four pounds, and I live four blocks from here. If you want to scramble after me, you're welcome."

Damn. No coat and no time. Still I said, "Sure," like I could think of no better pastime than a stroll in forty-five degrees, under a thick gray sky.

"What do you think of Second Home?" My words exploded into little puffs of smoke.

"You expect to get information with an anemic question like that? Good luck, sister. Fine, Second Home's just fine. Next."

The lady was scrambling toward Fifth Avenue as if Kevin Costner himself was waiting there for her, in the buff.

"Do you trust Karen Alexander?"

She stopped suddenly, pivoted on her gum-soled heel. "You know something about her, I want to hear it now, and not on the nightly news." Her hot breath felt good on my face.

I smiled. "Ma'am, I'm just trying to assess the center, to protect women like you."

She snorted. I didn't have to be a mind-reader to know what she was thinking. "Stupid city worker."

She took off again. The woman had to be a race walker. I scurried after her. We caught up with and passed the eagle-nosed postal worker I had knocked into earlier. He pulled to one side and watched us race by. I winked at him, but the guy didn't smile.

"Have you been using Second Home long?" I asked.

"Long enough." There was a funny sound coming from her jacket. I looked down. Sophie had this singsong mantra going full-speed, a tune littered with strange vowels and utter contentment. I couldn't blame her. The kid was nestled between her mom's full, warm breasts, while I was doing a quick-step, cold air burning the back of my throat.

I decided to try a different tactic. "Sophie's adorable. How old is she?"

My companion beamed. "Thirteen months. And she's absolutely brilliant." A quick glance my way. "Do you have children?"

"One. Unfortunately not so brilliant." Another lie, but hey, I go with what works.

Her pace eased up. She said, "Sorry," in a tone that would have rankled me if I really did have a kid who happened to be a tad slow.

"Thanks," I replied half-heartedly. "Now, please tell me you're an at-home mom who spends twenty-four hours a day stimulating her child with computer games and creative tasks, like transforming corn husks into Egyptian goddesses."

A nice laugh. She said, "I'm a single mom, so the answer unfortunately is no. I don't have the luxury of staying home all day. I teach at Brooklyn College, Psych one-oh-one, morning classes. But I do my best by Sophie. You should try reading *How to Have a Brilliant Child in Ninety Minutes a Day*. The techniques really work."

I checked out the prodigal child. She had drool

and some cheesy stuff eking from her mouth and her
cantaloupe tresses were pinched and projecting like
the Eiffel Tower from her incredibly round head. I
wondered if this was what brilliance resembled at
thirteen months.

Mrs. DeVine paused for a traffic light. "Tell me
the truth. Is there a problem at the center? Everyone
there looked pretty intense. And the city is such a
bureaucratic mess, I can't believe you're here to
check out a center with only eight children unless
there is a serious problem."

I smiled to acknowledge her deductive skills. She
seemed pleased. "Okay," I said, "but please keep this
under your hat."

She nodded earnestly.

"I brought my son here yesterday afternoon,for
the first time, and he came home with a mark above
his ribs. Karen and Livy said that he fell on a Tonka
toy. Maybe I'm just being too cautious, but I'm really
concerned about the type of care the children get at
Second Home. I mean, what kind of woman hires
someone like Olivia to watch over infants."

Mrs. DeVine laughed, squeezed my forearm.
"C'mon," she said, looking down the block for oncoming traffic. "Livy's a sweetheart. Most parents are
thrown by her appearance at first, but believe me,
she's incredible with the children. She hovers over
those babies as if they were her own."

My ears prickled. "Maybe that's the problem.
Maybe she loves them too much."

"First of all, that's just not possible. At this age,
children need all the love and attention they can get.
And second, Livy's really quite grounded. Matter of
fact, one of the reasons I chose Second Home is

because of her. You *do* know she's at Pace, for a night-study program in pediatric nursing. Really." She stopped suddenly in front of an apartment building. "This is where we part."

"What about her personal life?"

She shrugged. "Who knows? I think she may be bi. One week she's raving about some guy she met at a rock club in the city, and the next she's showing off pictures of her and some dykey-looking woman she went hiking with in Vermont. Honestly, I couldn't care less. All that matters is how she treats Sophie. And she does that just fine."

"Do you know anything about Karen's husband?"

"Miss Elusive? No. She keeps her personal life under wraps. To tell you the truth, at first I suspected she was gay. She has that, I don't know, Ida Lupino-as-prison-guard energy. Which is okay with me," she added hastily. "I've tried to draw her out a few times, but she always clams up. She's very intense, but I have no reason to suspect that she's anything but the consummate professional she seems to be. If you find out differently, please let me know." We exchanged phone numbers and then she unzipped her parka and said, "Say bye-bye, Sophie." I waited a full minute. I don't know how you judge IQ at that age, but apparently brilliance didn't extend to salutations. I didn't get so much as a finger lift or even a spitty gurgle.

I ran the whole way back to the center. The place was hopping. Whoever had planned this kidnapping knew what they were doing. There were too many people coming and going for me to get an accurate fix on anyone. I stood off to one side of the waiting area, analyzing expressions, looking for edginess, an

31

unexpected bead of perspiration on a chill day, an unnaturally pronounced greeting, anything, but all I got were parental goo-goos and angst.

One black-garbed woman had arrived to drop off her baby, and another woman was picking hers up. But my attention quickly snapped to the olive-skinned man. He wore a calf-length black wool coat that looked as if it had never been touched by inclement weather. Or a spitty infant, for that matter. He pushed between the two mothers and hurriedly handed a pink sack of baby flesh to Olivia. Their exchange was curt. Karen smiled at him and apologized profusely for having to leave the room "for a second" to fetch the pick-up. I had never seen Karen act, well, *mincing* was the word that sprung to mind. Her atypical demeanor didn't go unnoticed by the two mothers, whose mouths simultaneously puckered at the preferential treatment the guy was getting. I got a headache just watching all of them.

I signaled to Beth as she edged into the room. She came over with Carol, who was clutching a bottle of formula with a fierce possessiveness.

"Who are these people?" I asked.

"Parents."

"Pure genius, Beth. I mean, what do you know about them?"

Just then Karen reappeared with an infant clad in a black-and-white striped jumper. Beth aimed her chin at the woman who was now buckling Zebra Boy into a retro-style stroller. The woman had long salt-and-pepper tresses, nicely permed, and wore a black sweater, black slacks and black boots. "That's Joyce Gass. She's an editor at *Natural Times*, you know the magazine. Green power to the extreme.

She's somewhat of a loner, works at home in the afternoons. Drops Graham off a few minutes after we bring in Carol, but never stays long enough to chat. The other woman who's talking to Karen now —"

I shifted my attention. Now *she* was worth checking out. Gorgeous light brown skin, as smooth as coffee ice cream. Big black eyes, curly lashes. Her hair was bobbed and wind-blown. She was about five-foot-five, slim, with a quick smile as potent as a lighthouse blink on a clear night. "Whoa," I said spontaneously.

"Down, girl. She's spoken for. Her name's Yvette Santana. And her lover is equally striking. Her little girl's Zoe. A real sweetheart. I've never seen her in a bad mood."

There was envy in her voice that she didn't have to explain to me. I adore Carol, but my goddaughter's a heavyweight wailer.

"Any chance either woman could be involved in this?"

Beth pinched her lips pensively. "Pretty unlikely, I'd think. Whoever did this probably needs money, right? Well, Joyce is fairly comfortable, so I can't imagine that that would be a motive for her. On the other hand, she *is* very political, a radical environmentalist and animal rights advocate, and you know the latest on Oscar Roth."

Beth was crediting me with greater knowledge than I had. All I knew about Phyl's parents was that they owned Oscar's, a nationwide chain of super-markets, and were extremely wealthy. I asked Beth to elaborate.

"I guess Phyl didn't show you the blurb in last week's *New York* magazine?" I said no. "I'm not surprised. It focused on how New York's wealthiest families are pouring money into these horrible companies. It specifically mentioned how much the Roths have invested in that upstate lab that's using animals to test cosmetic and pharmaceutical products."

"The one that burned out rabbits' eyes with some new high-test dandruff shampoo?"

"That's it. The day after that issue hit the newsstands, I caught Joyce looking at Phyllis like she was the daughter of Satan."

Joyce and her son rolled out after Yvette Santana, leaving us alone with Mr. Expensive Wool Coat, who was rapidly issuing instructions to Olivia and Karen.

"What about him?" I asked.

"Got me." A look of consternation swept over Beth's face. She asked, "How old do you think that baby is?"

I checked out the kid in Olivia's arms. Wrapped tightly in a pink blanket, she was about the size of one of my cats. To my eyes, she resembled a newborn. I said as much to Beth, who just shook her head. Just then Carol decided she wasn't getting enough attention. She spiked her bottle across the room with a move that would've made Joe Montana proud. Beth sighed and went to retrieve it, while I moved over to the threesome near the hallway.

"What a precious little bundle," I said, sounding like someone from the South who watched daytime television for a living. If the human anatomy permitted self-butt-kicking, I would have done so. Twice.

The father turned to me, impatience in every line

34

of his acne-scarred face. He was stocky and thin-lipped and a good six inches taller than my five-nine. "Look," he snapped. "I don't have the time or inclination to make small talk." He scratched his chin with a manicured hand. The gesture sounded like a nail file scraping sandpaper.

My venom changed directions. I now ached to kick the butt of this cretin who spoke to me with the utter disdain of a successful businessman for what he assumed to be a lowly housewife.

"Are you a regular here?" I asked in my best Marabel Morgan voice. "I haven't seen you before." Karen shot me a warning look, while Olivia flashed me a conspiratorial wink.

The guy addressed Karen. "Who is she?"

I stopped the mistress from answering for me. "Robin Miller," I said, thrusting my hand in front of his barrel chest. "And you are?

He couldn't help himself. He shook my hand and said, "Edison Graves." Business habits die hard.

"Stockbroker?"

His eyebrows pulled together. I like to think of myself as a hardass, but that black-eyed stare of his burned through me in under five seconds. I blinked, the son of a bitch smiled, then turned his attention back to Karen.

"My wife's acting like this goddamn flu could kill her. I told her I'd make the drop-off, but there's no way I can pick Kirsty up at six, so one of you will have to bring her to my place. I want her there no later than six-fifteen. Sharp. She's on a strict schedule and I don't want it screwed up."

Olivia's right nostril flared, raising her another

notch in my esteem. "Oh," she said, "one of the babies in back is crying. Sorry, must run." She spun on her heel. The fact that the room monitor wasn't emitting so much as a burp wasn't lost on Edison Graves.

To Karen, he said, "I don't pay you good money so that Kirsty can be handled by some piece of English trash."

I started to open my mouth, but before I could Beth kicked the back of my calves. "Need you in the kitchen. Now." She herded me through the hallway.

"Let me practice my tae kwon-do on him, puh-lease," I wailed as we entered the kitchen. "One blow to the solar plexus."

"This is not your business, Robin." She placed Carol into a highchair. Our darling little terror was kicking up a storm. I went to help and she speared her bottle toward me. I got it in the thigh.

"When's she trying out for the Giants?"

Beth groaned. "She's picking up on our tension, Rob. We've really got to get home. Dinah still doesn't know what's going on. I haven't wanted to call her out of session, but she's going to worry if I'm not there by three." I checked my watch and realized Beth was right. I know their schedule better than my own. Dinah would be out of session in fifteen minutes and expect to see her family at home, eager for the ninety minutes they reserve each day for private playtime.

"Go on," I said. "Go home."

She hesitated. "You sure?"

I nodded.

My friend sighed. "Phyl's in the middle room.

God," she said, her eyes filling again. "I don't know how she's managing."

I had to leave the comforting to Dinah. "Take Carol and get out of here."

She wiped her eyes with a piece of paper towel. I picked the shreds off her blouse, kissed a damp cheek, then lifted Carol from the high chair. Her tiny feet were hidden in mini-Reeboks. One of them crunched into my chin.

For some reason, Beth and I laughed. It gave me the strength I needed to go inside to Phyl.

She sat in a rocking chair in the corner, staring blindly at Olivia who was urging Zoe to smack a set of bongo drums with a plastic hammer.

I palmed her shoulder. "How're you doing?"

She rested her cheek on my hand and said, "I'm kind of numb."

I squatted beside her. "What happened with your parents?"

She shuddered. "They wanted to call the Chief of Detectives, the Mayor's office and God knows who else. I went ballistic. Finally, they agreed to do this my way. You know why they gave in?"

"No."

"Publicity. My father doesn't like to see his name in the news unless it's in *The Wall Street Journal* under the headline 'Oscar's Stock Soars.' "

I had never heard Phyllis sound so bitter. But then again, I had never heard her talk about her parents before.

"They agreed to pay the ransom?"

"Oh, yes. I'm their only daughter, which makes Michael the sole male heir to my father's throne. I'm not sure I could command such a high price tag, but Michael? My father would probably sell me *and* my mother if it would bring back his prince."

"How are they getting the money to you?"

"They didn't say. One of my father's accountants is handling the transaction. Oh, don't worry. He'll be discreet. When it comes to purchasing loyalty and politic silence, my father is a regular spendthrift."

"Do your parents know about my role in this?"

She started. "Of course not. You know I'm not out to them. If my father knew, he'd dump me in the Gowanus and go buy himself a new daughter, preferably one who was married and eager to breed. Ask Matthew. He knows what I mean."

My eyebrows arched. Pretty extreme reaction, I thought. I cleared my throat and said, "Phyl, I meant my involvement in the kidnapping."

"Oh . . . oh . . . yes, they do. In fact, hiring you was a significant factor in winning my father's acquiescence. I told him your fee was five hundred a day, plus expenses —"

I started to protest — our fee is a lot lower — but Phyl cut me off.

"He can afford to pay you top dollar. Besides, if you charged less than that, my father would question your professionalism. He's a strange duck. The kind of self-made man who thinks the world should bow at his feet to recognize his amazing accomplishments. It really pisses him off that my mother and I see him as just another neurotic, controlling male. Your assignment, by the way, is to bring home Michael *and* the money. At least, that's how Oscar sees it." She covered her eyes with both hands. "God, I hope

I'm doing the right thing," she murmured more to herself than to me.

What could I say? If it were up to me, right now I'd be percolating a pot of strong joe for the square-jawed boys from the FBI. "Phyl, I've got to ask you a few more questions."

She nodded dumbly.

"Have you noticed anyone following you around?"

"No."

"Hangups or strange phone calls?"

Another no.

"What about Matthew? How hard did he fight for custody?"

The tip of her tongue ran along her bottom lip. "Matthew's not much of a fighter. He's more of a roll-with-the-punches kind of guy. Besides, we both knew it had to be this way."

"Can you think of anyone who might have a grudge against either one of you, or maybe your father?"

She turned away from me with a little snort of disgust. "If I knew the answers to any of these questions, don't you think I would have told you already? No, no and no. I don't know who took Michael . . . all I know is that he's gone and I want him home. I don't need revenge or justice, or any of that crap. I just need my son, okay?"

"We'll find Michael. Don't worry." There was no response. Phyl stared past me, into some private hell of her own. I squeezed her hand and moved over to Olivia, who was blowing kisses over Zoe's stomach. "Are she and Kirsty the only kids you have in the afternoon?"

She glanced at a Swatch watch that looked as if it had been designed by someone recovering from a bad flashback to the psychedelic sixties. "No, we have two more coming in the next hour. Pina and Simon. Twins. Eleven months old and wicked crawlers."

Twins. Great. That reduced the total family count at the center by one. And I could eliminate Beth and Dinah. And Phyl. And probably the half-deaf, half-blind seventy-two-year-old landlady who lived upstairs from the center. That left five families, all with access to Second Home.

I flipped through my notes. "Do you remember exactly what Michael was wearing earlier?"

She gave me the details, then added, "I never did finish telling you about the bloke on the corner, did I?"

"The one with the boa?"

"No. The one who was pacing back and forth, cursing up a storm. Your height, I'd guess. Dark brown hair, slicked back. Real pointy chin. Called me a bulldagger, he did, then went and banged his hand against the lamp post. Not just once, mind you. Three times. Hard. It happened right as I was leaving for lunch. He was quite off his bird."

An armory in Park Slope had been converted into a homeless shelter a few years ago. Olivia's description could have easily matched twenty-odd individuals who regularly parade down Seventh Avenue, including one who opens the door for me at the Chemical automated teller I use. I asked her if she thought this guy came from the armory.

"Matter of fact, no. He was well dressed and he

wore a God-awful cologne. There was something familiar about him, but I couldn't place the face."

She finished her description just as the kitchen door swung open. Karen entered with Kirsty Graves. The kid's skin looked shriveled, like old orange peel.

"Is she okay?" I asked.

Olivia answered first. "She would be, with different parents."

"Oh, for crissake," Karen said, "you don't know what you're talking about." She placed Kirsty into a crib with new bedding and then lowered a mobile until it was within the baby's reach. An assortment of birds and bells in primary colors dangled enticingly above Kirsty's head. She stared but made no sound and didn't move to touch it.

My stomach kicked. "How old is she?"

"Seven months," Olivia said, clearly anticipating my response.

We exchanged looks. I'm no baby expert, but Kirsty's size, skin color and lack of affect unnerved me.

Karen snorted as if the two of us were idiots. "She was born premature, and she's had a number of respiratory illnesses. Otherwise, Kirsty is a very healthy, normal baby. And the Graveses are solid people."

"Real solid. Like bricks," Olivia muttered under her breath.

"Another comment like that," Karen warned in a tone that made me understand exactly why Olivia called her the mistress, "and I *will* consider Mr. Graves's suggestion."

I'd had enough of this bullshit. I said to Karen, "When the two of you are done, I'd like to see your files on the people who contract with Second Home."

She stabbed a finger at me. "Phyllis hired you. Not me."

I stormed over. In a voice geared for her ears only, I said, "Fuck you. Whoever took Michael knows this place far too well. They knew when the kids napped, when Olivia left for lunch and which kid could command a good price tag. And from the looks of your front door, they didn't bother breaking in. They walked in, snapped up Michael and walked out within minutes. Without you noticing a goddamn thing. Odds are, they had a key. Get it now? This smells like an inside job. So unless you're ready to confess, my best guess is that one of your clients snatched Michael. So when I say I want to see your files, your response isn't optional. I mean, get them this instant or I'll call in the feds so fast you and Phyl won't have time to blink."

"Robin, please don't talk to her like that."

I spun around. Phyl had walked over. "Can I talk to you alone?" she asked.

"Please do," Karen muttered under her breath.

I ignored her and followed Phyllis into the kitchen. She opened the refrigerator. The first rack held a battalion of bottles labeled by name and date. On the second shelf I glimpsed a blue Tupperware container bearing Michael's name and the word *kosher*. Phyl cleared her throat, leaned toward the bottom shelf and removed a bottle of Yoo-Hoo. "You could use this," she said, offering me my favorite drink as if I were an infant requiring a pacifier.

42

I took it with some reluctance. I didn't want her thinking I could be bought so cheaply.

A sad smile played around her lips. "You're so predictable."

"Thanks, babe. Now why'd you call me out here?"

"I think maybe you're too close to me and Michael to be able to handle this."

I took a swig of the Yoo-Hoo and said, "You're probably right. So let's call in the authorities."

She knelt in front of me and rubbed her palms along my thighs. It was the type of caress that usually drives me wild. Amazingly enough, it still did. I stopped her.

"I'm not saying I don't trust you to do the right thing, Rob. I'm just asking you to try to keep some balance in this. Karen's not our enemy."

"How do you know that, huh? Right now, everyone's suspect." My words hit me between the eyes. I took a deep breath and asked, "Where were you this morning, Phyl?"

She stood up so fast, she stumbled backward. "I can't believe you."

"If I were a fed or even a patrol cop, I'd be asking you these questions, so don't get so —"

"You're not a fed or a cop. You're my lover!"

Wrapping her arms across her chest, she started to sob. Astonishment locked me in place. Phyl had never called me her lover before, and the word sounded odd to my ears. Sure, we had been seeing each other for a few months, and most nights culminated in some pretty hot sex. But I had never thought of us as being lovers. After a moment, I moved over to her and took her into my arms.

Weeping against my clavicle, she whispered, "Don't you know how much I love you?"

I couldn't swallow. I wasn't ready for this. Especially not now. "Phyl, I'm sorry. Please." I held her at arm's length. "Please. Right now, we have to focus on Michael. Just answer my questions, and try not to take them personally, okay?"

She nodded, but her eyes were asking me questions I didn't want to answer any time soon.

"So where were you?" I repeated.

I watched her shuffle over to the sink, her movements stiff and unnatural. She focused on washing dishes with an intensity that betrayed how hard she was struggling to hold herself together. "You know that earache I've been complaining about? I went in to see one of the doctors Beth works with. Then I waited around for her so that we could walk over here together." She wiped her hands on a dish towel. "Are you going to question Beth and Dinah too?" she asked sarcastically.

The thought never would have crossed my mind before hearing Phyl's alibi, but now I surprised myself by answering, "Of course." What had this job done to me? I studied my notepad until my pulse steadied, then asked, "Have you talked to Matthew?"

She shook her head, then harumphed. "Guess he's a suspect too, huh, Miss Tracy?"

How could I explain to her that this was the way I had to work, that I couldn't afford to trust anyone? Even as the words ran through my head, I heard my therapist snickering. Just last night she had said to me, "Isn't it convenient to have a job that makes you view the world through a magnifying glass. So much safer to be an observer than a participant. What would happen, Robin, if you stopped suspecting people? Just imagine the possibilities."

Right now, the possibilities included a kidnapper leaving Michael for dead and skipping with a quarter-million dollars, and all because I failed to ask the right questions, suspect the right people. Screw the self-examination. I had a job to do.

"Yes," I said. "Matthew's a suspect. Have you talked to him?"

She averted her eyes and said, "I can't find him," so quietly I wanted to pounce.

"What do you mean?"

"He left work early today."

"Why?"

More muttering.

"Phyl," I repeated, "why did he leave work?"

She snapped at me. "He felt sick, okay?"

"Did you call his house?"

The air between us turned electric. I knew what her answer would be before she spoke. "He wasn't there. The guy he's seeing doesn't know where he is."

I glanced at the clock above the sink. Michael had been missing for over three hours. And I had less than forty-eight to find him. And now, I had to find his father.

Chapter 3

The fanciest thing in my office is the computer setup on my credenza. SIA had started out with one sorry computer, donated by a grateful client. Tony likes to say that the damn thing sprouted, Jack and the Beanstalk style, until now we have several laptop units and three hot-shit desktop systems, one each for me, my partner and our full-time researcher, Jill Zimmerman. There's a CPU tower with a built-in fax and modem tucked in the corner of my office, and in front of me, an upgraded CD-ROM drive, an intimidating seventeen-inch monitor, a laser printer and speakers that address me in a cloying voice I always expect to say, "Seventh floor, housewares." There were so many wires snaking over and around my desk that I felt like an exhibit at the Bronx Zoo. I tugged on a cord that had snared my desk chair and something exploded on my desk.

I ducked. "Jill! What's the hell is this?" I shouted so she could hear me across the hall.

She came running in. "Oh . . . that. Jeez, you scared me. It's a calculator with a built-in hidden camera."

"Real subtle. No one's supposed to notice that five-hundred megawatt flashbulb?"

"Oh. You can disable that." She flipped a switch.

"Does the thing actually calculate?"

From the corner of my eye, I caught a glimpse of her best I-ate-the-mouse grin. "Okay, so I went catalog crazy. Shoot me."

"I'll do better than that. Until further notice, you're working for me exclusively. I cleared it with Tony. Sit down."

I tickled my keyboard, turned around and did a double-take. Up until lunch today, Jill had salt-and-pepper hair that parted in the middle and broke gently over her shoulders. Now I was looking at a saucy redhead with a chin-length bob.

"You hiding from the law?" I asked. The words she mouthed at me weren't terribly polite. I grinned at her. "Very sexy."

"Like I could care," she said in return.

We have a great relationship. With all the piss and vinegar we emit, you'd never guess how much genuine affection we hold for each other. Until one of us is in trouble.

I ran through the day's events. Jill slumped among the throw pillows of my forest-green couch. "My God," was all she could say when I was done.

I glanced over my shoulder. My computer search had netted thirty-seven articles on the Alice Breen kidnapping. I downloaded them, then said, "Your reading material. I need to know if we're dealing with the same kidnapper. I want to know where, when and how. See if there's anything on the drop. Give me dialogue, names, addresses, everything you can find."

She leaned forward. "I could save time just by calling the day-care center where the Breen kid was taken."

"Duh. Of course, you could. The problem is we can't afford a leak. If you can concoct some fail-safe pretext for getting the information, fine, but I don't want anyone getting a whiff of a second kidnapping."

Incredulity twisted down the corners of her mouth. I knew the look, because I had been fighting the same expression all day long.

"Save your reservations for someone else. I don't have the time. Matter of fact, neither do you. I hope you've kept up your Evelyn Woods reading skills."

She stepped around my desk, hit a few keys and waited while an image slowly emerged. The screen crystallized into the cover of *Newsweek*, Desiree Breen collapsing into the arms of her red-eyed husband. They were standing in the living room of their brownstone, in front of a fireplace whose mantel displayed an array of framed photographs of a fat-cheeked baby girl, with designer dimples and a one-toothed smile that could break hearts. And did.

"That's where I should start," Jill said grimly.

I heard a ping behind me and swiveled around to find Tony clicking his class ring against the jamb. "Start there," he said. "And you might as well call *Newsweek* directly."

My partner looked like crap. What was left of his hair was cropped short, revealing a moonscape scalp. His sunken cheeks made his dark eyes seem unnaturally large. In the past week, the corners of his lips had become punctuated with small sores. The suit jacket he wore hung from his shoulder like a cape.

"We need to take you shopping, Tony," I said, without thinking.

There was a slight narrowing of his eyes, a deepening of the furrows on his forehead. "Why waste the money?"

My lips opened, but no words came to me. Jill coughed politely, then said, "Okay, Tony, so how would you approach this?"

Without breaking eye contact with me, he said, "I'd call in the experts, but since Miller's friend is as bull-headed as Miller, that's not an option. My next suggestion is to canvass the neighborhood. Go door to door, straight down the block. Talk to the other parents from Second Home. Grill that amazon bitch, Karen Alexander, and while you're at it, nail down Phyllis and her husband. Find out everything you can about what happened today, and compare the facts to the Breen case. I've already started a check on that English kid with the pierced nose. I can see her having some druggie friends interested in fast bucks. We also have to get ready for the follow-up call. We can't get an official tap on Phyllis's phone, but we can hook up one of those jobs from 'I Spy.' We should do the same at Second Home."

All the time he spoke, our eye contact remained unbroken. He was trying to tell me something he wasn't ready to vocalize and I wasn't ready to hear. We had played this game before. I stood abruptly. "You want in on this, Tony? 'Cause if you do, you'll have to settle for the back room. The kidnapper knows what you look like and, for some reason, he didn't think you were just another Park Slope progressive checking in on his kid, so you can't show your face anywhere near Phyllis or Second Home. Got it?"

He raised his chin at me, his basset-hound eyes a little glassy. Jill turned away. We all knew what was happening.

Tony rubbed his face wearily. "Don't boss me around, Miller. This is *my* agency." He spoke gruffly, but his words were bullshit. Tony was tired. It was time for me to move into the driver's seat and let my partner ride.

I said, "My girlfriend. My case. And these are the terms. You going to help me out or not?"

He shook his head, an elusive smile darting my way. "Sure. Without me, kid, you're diddly-squat. And Miller..." His eyes sparked. "I want this boy found alive, as much as...no...*more* than you. I want him alive." He squared off his shoulders and Jill and I exchanged expectant glances. He didn't let us down. "'Let us cast off the works of darkness, and let us put on the armor of light.' Romans something." Then in a quieter tone he added, "I really need this, Miller." He clicked his class ring against the door

50

again as if it were a bell signaling the next round. "Give me my assignment."

I switched gears, gave Tony the Breen research and Jill the job of checking up on the families from Second Home. I still hadn't located Phyl's husband, Matthew Brickman, so I dumped that task on Tony as well. The phone taps would have to wait until tomorrow.

Among the three of us, I was the best face-to-face liar so I took on the neighborhood canvass. For the next thirty minutes or so, I played Dr. Frankenstein with myself. I had an overnight bag packed with clothes that would best suit different personas — bag lady, nurse, businesswoman and Jehovah's Witness. My desk contained an assortment of business cards. I've been a plumber, lawyer, insurance broker and a cellist at the Philharmonic. Tonight I needed to be especially creative, and flexible. I wrote down a variety of pretexts, assembled my flimflam kit, switched my Land's End briefcase for a leather attaché, and headed for the streets. Story number one: I was looking for the owner of a wallet found outside Second Home. The only clue I had was the picture of Michael tucked into a plastic sleeve. For added credibility, I decided to position myself as a neighborhood lawyer.

New York City isn't an easy town for liars. There are too many of us. People expect to be swindled, duped, ripped off and generally taken for a ride through hell. I started near the church on Fourth Avenue, the corner farthest from Second Home, where my chances of unearthing vital information were negligible. Good thing too. I had three doors slammed in my face. Being as sharp as a tack, I soon figured out that no one was buying my Good Samaritan story. No problem.

I became Diane Whitmore, legal counsel for American Society for Leukemia Research. My mission: to find one of two notorious con artists soliciting the good citizens of Park Slope for donations that never made it further than their pockets. This nefarious couple actually used their one-year-old son as a hook to tug on people's heartstrings, pretending that the poor boy was stricken with leukemia, lie, lie, lie.

Apparently, people were much more receptive to the idea that a grifter was circulating among them. I flipped an ID card, flashed a briefcase full of official ASLR publications, and told the New York suspicious types that they could verify my identity by calling an 800 number linked directly to my agency. Jill was primed and waiting. Amazingly, only eight people went that far to check me out. Most quickly hopped into my bullshit. Unfortunately, I had made it almost all the way up the block and still had found no one who had been contacted by my scam team — surprise, surprise — or had noticed any suspicious male or female with a baby in tow.

It was past nine-thirty and my feet throbbed horribly inside the stupid pumps I had chosen to wear as part of my personal Halloween trek. My nose was running and a little tickle had beamed into my throat from distant virus-space. I had three more brownstones to go, and I wanted to spit.

Instead I rang the next doorbell. The guy who answered the garden-level buzzer had thick, black hair slicked back, Forties style. His eyes were robin's egg blue, so large and luminescent I instantly felt on guard. A friend of Tony's who works as a sketch artist for the NYPD once asked me if a subject we were investigating had a heart-shaped face. At the time I laughed, instantly envisioning a walking, talking Hoyle playing card straight out of *Alice in Wonderland*. Now I understood what she meant. The guy had a broad forehead and his face dove into a pointy chin spotted with bristly hairs. The only thing that was missing was an arrow through his head. He listened to my story with polite interest, betraying his boredom with an occasional twitch of his right eyebrow and nervous stamp of his foot.

After a moment or two, he let me in. I followed him into the living room. After viewing a few dozen brownstones, I felt the same way I do after listening to an endless loop of Pachelbel's *Canon* while waiting for someone to take me off hold. All the layouts were essentially the same. Railroad flats with rooms leading into rooms leading into rooms. The bedrooms were in the back, overlooking the imprisoned squares of grass and trees us city folk like to refer to as nature. The kitchens were relegated to the middle of the apartment, usually in the form of a U punctuated by a bar demarcating the start of the "living room." Sure, there were variations. Second Home, for instance, broke tradition by housing the kitchen in the rear. But for the most part, the brownstones were variations on a theme. This place was no different.

The wood floors looked freshly sanded and polyurethaned, the windows were the new pull-in kind and the walls smelled like Benjamin Moore. His couch was far too large for the room, a beige sectional whose corner unit had mysteriously evaporated. In front of it sat a battered wood chest that looked as if it had once served a purpose nobler than holding up a cracked mug of dark coffee and a half-eaten loaf of Sara Lee's pound cake. My attention moved to a series of photographs lining two of three walls. At first I assumed they were bad examples of abstract art, *Exploration in Gray, Series Ten*, or some such nonsense. But as I looked an image emerged from the murky depths. Misty gray swirls settled into the shapes of owls perched on gnarled tree limbs, in three different seasons. At the core of each photograph pulsed silver pearls, the round owl eyes collecting moonlight.

I averted my eyes and said, "Nice place. Looks like you moved in pretty recently."

"Three weeks ago. I used to live on St. John's." He plopped onto the sofa, snatched up the remote and lowered the volume. A Hitachi television I recognized as a Seventies model was tucked into a non-working fireplace. We both stared at the screen as Oprah Winfrey and Michael Jackson strolled across his Santa Barbara ranch.

"Can you believe that guy?" he practically sputtered. "Tramp!"

My attention jerked back to my host. "Excuse me?"

He looked embarrassed. "I mean, he's just a . . . a . . ." His features contorted as he looked for the right word. "Nigger freak!"

Hello. I had clearly entered the bigot zone. I took a step back, felt a bead of moisture escape one nostril, paused long enough to grab a tissue from a box on the end table and then felt the zap. This guy was a dead-on match to Olivia's description of the man who had called her a bulldagger.

"Excuse me, Mr. —" What the hell was the name on the bell? Worthy? Washington?

"Wilmington. Elmore Wilmington. As in Delaware. Hey, I hope you're not upset. Sometimes words just pop out of my mouth. I don't mean anything by that word, not like you think."

"Look, I just have a few questions and then I'll . . ."

"Shit. Listen to him." Wilmington pointed at the set.

Michael Jackson was talking about John Merrick, the deformed creature known as the Elephant Man. "I love the story . . . it reminds me of me a lot. It made me cry because I saw myself in the story."

Wilmington snorted. "What the hell does he know, huh? Living in his fucking Neverland, millions of dollars socked away to keep his fantasies from breaking down." His head jerked four or five times in a row, then he slapped the chest almost as many times. "Nigger freak!" The man was clearly crazy. And the most likely suspect I had yet encountered. I sat down, my nerves on a slow sizzle.

"Mind if I watch a while?" I asked.

He faced me, just slightly startled, then nodded. "Fascinating, huh, how someone that bizarre can soar so high? When you got money, shit, nothing can stop you. Nothing." This time he kicked the chest so hard, his coffee mug skidded off and smashed into the floor. In response his right arm lurched forward, not in an effort to stop the mug from falling, but more like a karate chop. He punctuated the motion with another outburst, "Cunt!"

My teeth ground together. I felt more irritated than frightened. The guy was out of control. I found

55

myself wondering if he had the ability to mastermind a kidnapping.

He swept up the shards and, to his credit, shot me a flustered grin. "I'll be right back."

As soon as he left the room, I snapped into high prowl. I removed the loaf of pound cake and lifted the chest lid. My eyes widened. The inside was divided into rows and compartments, almost like a tool chest. The first tray held a series of razor-edged knives with handles that gleamed like the inside of a shell. I peeked underneath. At the bottom right sat a camera with an infrared zoom lens. I shifted it to one side and felt my breath catch in my throat. A thirty-eight rested at the bottom of the chest, wrapped in a chamois cloth. Just as I fingered the barrel, I heard footsteps shuffling my way. I started, dropping the lid with a smack that made my teeth chomp together. I took a deep breath and sat upright. Wilmington entered, kicked his heel against the wall like an impatient mule, started toward me, backed up and repeated the kick.

"Got an itch," he said, as if his words made sense.

A commercial came on and I stared at it, hoping I was the only one who could hear my heart thundering. I had a choice: make a fast exit or start my interrogation. Every nerve in my body said, "Get the hell out of here," but then I thought of Michael. My breath exploded from my lungs, where it had been trapped for close to a minute. Wilmington's focus was on me. His gaze was piercing.

I looked his way, clasped my hands in my lap to

still their trembling and repeated my line about the local con artists. He smiled the whole time. I couldn't tell if he knew I was lying or if he was just getting a kick from my company. He said no one had come around begging for his money, which he didn't have to give anyway. "Sounds like a great scam, though. Maybe I should give it a shot. Ha! Just kidding . . . you should've seen your face. But no, to answer your question, no, I didn't see a phoney fundraiser running around this block with a kid in tow. And I should know. I'm home all day. Lunch time, I'm outside with my bongo drums. The rest of the afternoon, I'm inside, painting. I'm an artist. Acrylics. My studio's in the back if you want to see."

I said sure. He went first and I curled my hands into fists just in case he decided to attack. The apartment was a pure shotgun: room led into room in a straight, unbroken line. He pushed aside the heavy, painted French doors and we passed into a narrow, windowless alcove that served as a bedroom. There was a mattress on the floor, with knotted blankets draped along one side as if someone had flung them off suddenly in a fit of sleepless frustration. The only other piece of furniture was a scarred oak dresser whose top was littered with newspapers and cheap colognes. As I walked by, I noticed a *New York Times* from a few months ago. A blurb on the Breen kidnapping trailed down the third column. My focus snapped forward. Wilmington's entire body was jerking as if he were suffering an epileptic spasm. He spun rapidly and latched onto me so fast I didn't have time to jump back.

"Dagger!" he spat into my face.

I tried to shrug out of his grasp, but his hands were astoundingly powerful.

I screamed, "Let me go!" and kicked his shin hard.

It was as if a rubber band had snapped. He released his vise-hard grip all at once and I stumbled backward.

"Sorry. Sorry. I just remembered I have to call a friend of mine. His name's Dagger. Sorry."

The odd part was he looked truly repentant. I knew I should hightail it out of there while I still could, but this guy was the closest I'd come to a real suspect and I wasn't about to let him slip away.

I shrugged, as if it were all in a day's work.

He looked puzzled, then grinned and said, "Go on in while I make this call. I'll be right back." He parted the sliding doors and I entered a chilly room with large windows and a glass door leading into the rear garden. The room felt cavernous. Ambient light drifted in from the apartment building on the next block, passed through the bare limbs of trees and etched the wood floor with strange swaying motions. "The switch is on the wall," Wilmington said. The doors scratched into place, leaving me standing alone in darkness.

A shiver ran through me. I could almost hear my partner chiding me for letting myself get trapped like this. Wilmington could be calling in his cohorts and here I was stranded in his studio like a turkey sticking its neck out for the slaughter. I found the switch and flipped it. Bright, white light showered down from an expensive-looking halogen fixture.

Whatever else Wilmington might be, one thing

was certain. He really was an artist. Two easels were positioned by the windows, separated by an oak stool with a revolving seat. The easels faced each other so that the artist could spin back and forth between the two as if they were snare drums. The images on the canvases mirrored Wilmington's odd jerkiness, with clashing colors and bold strokes, the visual equivalent of funky jazz. One wall was lined with finished canvases sealed into some sort of stretching device that looked as if it could double as a sex toy for the Marquis de Sade. The other wall held several pieces of red clay pottery from which brushes spouted like wildflowers. Lining the lowest shelf was a row of mason jars gleaming with brilliant paints. The wall itself was art.

I moved closer to examine the finished paintings. At first I assumed the art was abstract, non-representational celebrations of movement and light, but as I continued to scrutinize the canvas an image unexpectedly coalesced. Hidden inside the twirl of color and fluid shapes was a portrait of a man grasping a little girl tight to his chest. They sat astride a carousel horse as a whirlwind spun around them.

Wilmington appeared next to me. "You see them, don't you?"

I stared at him, gulped, then said, "It's very powerful."

"Nothing's as powerful as the grip of children."

Oh shit. Lead him to the water, I warned myself. "Do you have kids of your own?"

Now he glared at me. "What do you think?" His tone was angry, as if I had just insulted him. He flipped off the light. Suddenly blind I stumbled away from the hiss of his steady breathing. He was close, too close. No matter where I moved, he was near me. I could feel the heat of his body behind me. I spun around, knocked my shin into an easel leg. His hands were on me again, pulling me toward him. My eyes regained focus and I caught the hunger in his eyes. I twisted away.

He said, "Let's go back inside."

I followed at a comfortable distance. When we got back in the living room, Oprah was still at it with Michael Jackson. I focused on the TV with relief. The mundane never seemed so appealing. She asked Jackson if he was still a virgin and both of us laughed out loud. The sound eased the tension. I figured it was a great time to exit. "Look, I appreciate your time, Mr. Wilmington."

"Right. I'm sure I helped your investigation." His inflection made me stop. The guy might be crazy, but he wasn't stupid. I got the sense he knew I suspected him of something. He slapped his cheek abruptly, then pointed to the set. "Get her."

Brooke Shields had on her thick-browed, sincere look. She said, "Can you blame him for wanting to be surrounded by the innocence and purity of children? The light in their eyes is what he wants to keep alive in his own soul."

"What does he know about light?" Wilmington growled. His nostrils flared. "Baby, it's cold out there," he said, then choked off the rest of his words. His attention returned to me. "Better bundle up. This weather can kill you."

* * * * *

It was too late to finish the neighborhood canvass, so I decided to head back. In the past hour, the temperature had plummeted and strong gusts had begun sweeping down from the direction of Prospect Park. I'm no lightweight, but I had to angle my body and forcefully shoulder myself into the wind to avoid being pushed back down the block. I worried that Wilmington's words might be prophetic. The cold bit into my exposed skin, curled into my nostrils and chafed my lips. I sneezed so hard once that my back spasmed. The fifteen-minute walk to my office took at least a week. When I got there, the lights were blazing and the aroma of fresh-brewed coffee beckoned to me from behind the closed door. I felt like Noah sniffing the first scent of earth. I stepped inside with enormous relief.

Tony was in my office, handing Phyllis a mug. She stabbed a cigarette against the sole of her shoe, then raised her eyes my way. "Thank God you're back."

"I didn't know you smoked." The words were out before I could stop them.

She looked at me from under raised eyebrows. "I'm a *little* stressed right now, Rob." The sarcasm was well earned.

"Sorry." I sat beside her and kicked off my shoes.

Tony tapped me on the shoulder. "Before you take off any more apparel, I'd like to see you outside."

I kissed Phyl's hand and then joined Tony in his office. He closed the door behind me and said, "You've got to talk sense into your friend. She's refusing the phone tap. I don't mean this as an insult, kid, but she can't put all her faith in you and you alone. A kidnapping is a highly volatile situation. You've got to work hard to tip the odds in your favor and we don't have the manpower. The FBI would have a dozen men on this, minimum, and meanwhile Phyllis is pissed you called in me and Jill. This is nuts."

"I'll talk to her."

"Do more than that. Convince her."

"I'll try." I dove for a tissue just as another sneeze racked my body. "Did you have any success finding her husband?"

"Yeah. He got home about two hours ago. Seems he was out shopping for a birthday present for his new boyfriend. I said, very nice, bring me the receipts. He said the trip wasn't a success. Couldn't even remember all the stores he'd been in. I'll give him this, though. The last thing he said was, 'Do whatever you can to get my son back.' I bet you if he was the one calling the shots, we'd be hauling in the feds."

"Maybe I'll call him myself."

"He won't be there. Said he's been staying with his boyfriend. But he wouldn't give me the guy's name. Gave me some cockamamie line about how his boyfriend's so in the closet he sleeps with hangers. I don't mind telling you, Rob, this case is a ball buster."

"If you've got balls, which I don't." I made another beeline for the Kleenex and blew my nose. "Why don't you call it a day, Tony? We'll start fresh in the morning."

He shrugged and went for his coat. I was almost

out of his office when I became conscious of the increasing rawness at the back of my throat. I said, "I think I'm getting a cold, so I may sleep in tomorrow. Maybe I'll even work from home."

Tony slammed the coat rack against the wall so hard that it rebounded and spiked into the back of the leather chair facing his desk. I stared at the rack as if it were a prop from the set of *Poltergeist II*.

"Cut the crap, Miller. I don't need your fucking protection! Okay? Turn around and face me." His skin was a mottled red. A pearl of spit clung to the corner of his lips. "I'm dying. Dying. Not ten years from now. Not even twelve months from now. I know it and you know it. My bowels are shot . . . everything I eat shits right out of me . . . not that I enjoy eating any more. Some mornings I lay in bed and touch my body like it was someone else's. Whose fucking ribs are these?" His fists knocked into his chest with a hollow thud. "I've gotten so thin, I can count each goddamn bone in my body. Do you get it? I won't, I *can't* play this game anymore. I don't have the energy. If you can't handle my sickness, then get the fuck out of the business. You're no son-of-a-bitch angel of death or whatever crap you've been pinning on yourself to keep yourself safe and far from the rest of us mortals. You've got a cold and I've got AIDS. Big, fucking deal. You think it makes a difference to me if I get sick today or next week, huh? 'Cause it doesn't. It doesn't." He swallowed hard. "What matters to me is that minutes before they cart me away, I'm doing something real. I'm alive, engaged and maybe even saving someone's life. So save your fucking pity for someone else."

A tremor loped through me. I took a step forward. "Okay, Mr. Rough-and-Tumble, want to French kiss?"

His jaw dropped and eyes widened. "What..." And then one corner of his mouth curled up. He swept his coat from the floor and righted the coat rack. "You really are nuts," he said with affection. "Tell you what ... take two aspirins and call me in the morning."

I painted on a smile until I heard his footsteps on the outer stairs, then I crumbled into his leather desk chair. Phyllis found me there, taking deep breaths.

"What the hell was that about?" she asked. Her palm locked onto the door jamb. The tension running through her body was almost imperceptible, except on her lips. They were thin and tremulous, with tiny blood blisters where she'd been gnawing on them all day.

I stood up. "Nothing, just some friction between me and Tony."

"Why do you put up with him? You don't need a partner, especially not a creep like him."

With more annoyance than I expected, I said, "I like him, Phyl. That's why he's my partner."

"Oh..." She cut the distance between us by half. "Sorry ... I guess I've been acting like a shit, haven't I?"

I shook my head. "I'm amazed you're able to stand upright."

"Only because I have you." She folded my arms

around her, then rested her head on my shoulder and sighed heavily. "I'm doing the right thing, Robin, I know it."

I chinned a path through her hair and kissed her. "You have to let us place the taps, Phyl."

Before I knew it, she had pushed herself back an arm's length. "And what happens if these kidnappers are as technologically sophisticated as you and can detect it? What then? You and your partner say, 'Oops, sorry your son's dead but, hey, we tried.' Goddamn, we are going to do this my way. The kidnappers get their ransom and I get my son. Period." Her gaze careened around the room. "Doesn't anyone around here smoke?"

I watched as she patted herself down. It was time to play hardball. "Phyl." She ignored me. I repeated her name.

"*What?*" She found a butt in her pocket and headed back to my office for a light.

I followed her in, waited for the tip of the cigarette to catch, then said, "If you don't agree to the taps, I'm calling in the feds." The smoke curled around her eyes, which flashed at me with ire. She was reaching the breaking point. I decided, what the hell and poked an ashtray at her. "And put that goddamn thing out."

For a second I expected her to sock me across the room, but instead she caved. She stabbed out the cigarette like she was crushing a cockroach. "Can you guarantee that the tap won't be detected?"

"No. But right now it's our best chance for

getting a bead on whoever took Michael. I'll have Jill set them up first thing tomorrow. You should probably let Karen know, okay?"

She nodded, said, "I know you're trying to help," and then unexpectedly her mouth was on me. She tasted ashy and I found myself pulling back, but she didn't let go. Her kiss became deeper, more insistent.

Despite myself, I began to respond. I knew what she was doing. I've done it plenty of times myself. Sex as Novocain.

She tugged off my suit jacket, pressed me against the desk, her mouth migrating to my earlobe, sucking, pleading. "Make me forget, baby, please, for a little while. Take me out of my head." Her hands yanked up my shirttails, ran along my back and plucked the hooks of my bra. Moist palms traced the line of my torso, clutched my waist as she lowered her head and pulled greedily on my nipples. Her flame caught me. I groaned out loud, feeling my body clutch, desperate for fingers, tongue. I opened my shirt, then hers and we rocked against each other, knees interlocked, an erotic battle for dominance. She undid my zipper, rubbed me through my underpants until the ache became unbearable. I flipped us around, backed her onto the desk and lifted her ankle-length skirt up around her hips. She was already naked underneath. I chuckled to myself. These religious women are something else.

An hour later we lay intertwined on my couch. Phyl was fast asleep. It was after midnight and, as usual, I was wide awake. To make matters worse, my throat felt scratchy. I untangled myself and fetched my clothes. My office smelled like sex and I felt empty. I glanced at Phyl. She looked incredibly vulnerable, her pale skin exposed to harsh fluorescent light. I draped her skirt over her back, then exited my office.

Michael was still out there somewhere, possibly cold and hungry, probably frightened, but at least alive — or so I hoped. I doubted the kidnappers would harm him before receiving the money. Most kidnap victims insist on proof their child is unharmed before capitulating to a ransom demand and I intended to make sure Phyl did the same. The void I felt inside, though, had little to do with Michael's disappearance.

Phyl had called me her lover. And I wasn't in love.

There are times I fear that something inside me, some neuron essential to appropriate emotional response, had disconnected back when I was a child. I scuffed into Jill's office and tucked myself into her velveteen club chair without bothering to turn on the light. Her printer was still on, emitting a green glimmer and enveloping the room in a steady, soft hum. I felt as if I were hidden inside the curl of a conch. I hugged my knees to my chest and lowered my head. How had I gotten here?

When I was just three years old, I accidentally shot and killed my sister Carol. Her death transformed me and my family. After his initial outbursts of fury, my father never again spoke directly to me, holding fast even on his deathbed. My mother — dear, tight-lipped mom — raised me with an emotional distance I have not yet learned to cross. Maybe I never will. Oh, I've come close. The eight months I spent with copper-haired K.T. Bellflower were the best in my life. Passionate, humorous and steadfast, K.T. had offered me a glimpse of

Shangri-la. But then again, Shangri-la ain't exactly a place you can buy plane tickets to. I still don't fully understand why the relationship came crashing down around me. My therapist and best friends like to point out the fact that as soon as the relationship hit rough roads, I was out shtupping some other woman. I smiled grimly. Maybe they had a point. Not that I planned to admit that out loud to anyone any time in the near future. A girl has to protect her pride.

All of a sudden, the overhead light flipped on. I flinched against the harsh glare. Phyl asked me if I was all right and I found myself unable to make eye contact with her. I said yes, then explained I couldn't afford a night off. Not with Michael gone. She draped her arms around me. "I'm not expecting you to be a hero. Besides, what can you do tonight?" Her words were meant to be comforting, but her tone was expectant. Was there something I really could accomplish tonight?

"What does Matthew do for a living?" I asked.

"He's a clown."

"Phyl, I'm serious. What does he do?"

"*He's a clown.* A bona fide, crab-apple-nosed, frizzy-haired clown. He started out doing these stints at neighborhood parties. You know, sort of dial-a-clown? Now he works at this place in Chelsea where parents can dump their kids for a few hours and not feel guilty because, after all, wouldn't the kids rather be entertained by a clown who juggles than hang out with their dull, middle-class folks all day."

I straightened up just as Phyl moved to curl up in my lap. "What kind of a relationship does he have with your parents?"

"You're joking, right? How do you think they feel?

My father's father earned a living hauling ice around Williamsburg, eighteen hours a day, six days a week. My dad started out working at a corner grocery store, the kind that still had sawdust on the floors, and yet by forty he had amassed his first million. Matthew will be lucky if he can afford cat food when he retires. How do my parents feel about him? He's a loser. You wouldn't believe how supportive they were when I told them we planned to divorce. They didn't even care that I was pregnant. My father thinks he's finally going to get himself a son-in-law of worth." She squirmed into my lap and tugged on my earlobe. "Little does he know what surprises I have in store for him."

I shrugged her off and stood. "What about Matthew's boyfriend?"

"He's an architect . . . and I see where you're going. Matthew would never put Michael at jeopardy. And Justin wouldn't hurt a fly."

"But they could use the money. A quarter-million dollars is a nice cushion, by anybody's standards. Where does Justin live?"

She refused to give me the address.

"Phyl, they could be behind this. At the very least, I have to question them."

"Justin comes from a very religious family. No one knows he's gay."

"Then how'd he meet Matthew?"

"At the gay community center, on Thirteenth."

"So he's not that closeted, is he?"

"Listen, he has family members who are Lubavitch. Do you understand? They are *beyond* orthodox. This is a community that ostracizes people who *date* outside the religion."

"So he'd rather live a lie than lose his family?" I snapped.

She planted her hands on her hips. "Not everyone is as eager as you are to cut off family ties, Robin."

Stab the knife in and turn. I didn't need this shit. Blood pounded in my ears as I asked for Justin's last name.

"Why the hell does that matter?"

"It matters."

"Kleinbaum."

I said thank you and sashayed around her. She didn't bother following me into my office.

She yelled at me from the hallway. "Look, we're both on edge, so I'm going home for a while. When you're ready to collapse into my arms, that's where I'll be." And then, right before the door closed, she said, "I love you, Robin Miller, no matter what."

The coffee in my mug had filmed over. I sloshed it around, waiting until I heard the downstairs door, then proceeded to get myself a fresh cup of joe. Truth be told, when it came to finding Michael, Phyl was in my way. And for now, the case was more important than our relationship. But wasn't that always my way? For an instant, I thought again of K.T. and how I had allowed a murder investigation to overcome my focus then as well.

The coffee tasted burnt and lukewarm. Still I downed two cups before returning to my computer. I was still online. I dialed into Identifier USA and typed in Justin's name. In less than a minute I had his address. Adrenaline took over. I rummaged in my closet for a pair of black jeans and a dark shirt and then I stripped with something akin to glee. Fuck everyone and everything. Robin Miller was on the hunt.

Chapter 4

Justin Kleinbaum lived on the Upper West Side, not far from my sister, Barbara. I knew I had a problem as soon as I saw the building. It was one of those prewar buildings stretching along West End Avenue for the equivalent of two city blocks. The building probably housed more people than you'd find in the average Midwest town. I wasn't worried about finding the right apartment. Identifier had yielded all the information I needed, with one important exception: how to bypass the lanky doorman lurking beyond the second set of glass doors. I couldn't wreak havoc with the buzzers without him seeing me. And I didn't want my arrival formally announced.

I raised the hood of my jacket against the cold and circled the building. On the side that faced West 76th Street I found a gray steel door with a vestige of graffiti someone had tried to erase. It could lead to a garage, an inner staircase or the super's quarters. I watched it for a good twenty minutes. Finally, finally, when stamping my feet no longer brought even the illusion of warmth and each swallow felt as if it held shards of broken glass, a young man exited from the door. He ran across the street to a liquor store, emerged with a squat bottle in a plain paper bag and then reentered the building through the same door. I strode over and took a good look at the lock. Lucky for me, the owners of the building were security-handicapped. It was a fairly standard pin tumbler lock. My brother's a locksmith in Staten Island who spent a good part of his teen years breaking and entering. He's taught me a lot. I whipped out my Scorpion III+, a handy-dandy pick machined from aircraft grade aluminum. My palm tight around the rubber grip, the baby went in smooth, did a little battery-powered jig and snapped the lock in less than fifteen seconds.

Justin lived on the sixteenth floor and I had no desire to tax my lungs. I hopped up two flights, then searched out the elevator. An elderly man with a fuzz cut and a Fu Manchu smiled at me as the doors opened. A rainbow wool scarf circled his neck. All at once he unraveled it with dramatic flair, like a cowboy flourishing a lasso. "Dahling," he said, "this winter thing has got to be dealt with. Suggestions?"

"Move to Key West."

He cackled, snatched my wrist and said, "My point exactly! Try convincing Frederick, please."

"Frederick?"

"Frederick McCutcheon. Former fireman . . . ooh." He fanned himself with his hand. "My, my. He is still a specimen." Wink, wink. "The man is in love with New York City, imagine. If it were up to me, we'd be in Florida right this minute, sipping Blue Whales and squishing sugar-white sand between our toes. But no . . . my Frederick prefers New York." He rolled his eyes. "Who are you visiting, sweetheart? Tell me it's that darling femme on eighteen?"

I corrected him and he looked disappointed. "A man? And one I don't know? This is not promising. Not at all." The elevator halted on fourteen. He stepped through and slapped the doors as they began to close. "If he's a bore . . . and he must be, darling, if *I* don't know him . . . come down and join me and Frederick for a drink. We'll be up for hours and adore the company of other night creatures. And you're so adorable, we'll just pretend you're a boy."

His laugh followed me up the shaft. It sounded like, "Ahh, arf, arp." I felt sad when it disappeared.

Justin's apartment was six doors down from the elevator. It was after one in the morning. A good time to catch prey off guard. I rang the buzzer and waited. The first sound I heard made my heart pump harder. A child's cry wailed through the apartment and was quickly silenced. If Michael was in the apartment . . . I wrenched the Scorpion pick from my pocket and stabbed it into the lock. Almost instantly the door opened. The man standing there in his Jockey underwear looked at me, looked at the pick in my hand, then screamed, "Justin, call the police! Now!"

I acted fast. "Name's Robin Miller. I'm dating your ex-wife."

He stared at me with arched eyebrows. The expression was almost comical, except clearly neither of us felt like laughing. "Forget it, Jus! Believe it or not, it's Phyl's new squeeze." Then to me, "Should I let you in or do you prefer breaking and entering?"

"B and E is a lot more fun, but since the door's open, what the hey?"

He moved aside and waved me in with a wave of his fingers. Justin stood dead center of the living room, a baby grasped to his chest with one hand, a phone in the other. He too was naked except for a pair of blue-and-white boxers spotted with little multicolored menorahs. Clearly a Channukah present. He was a tiny man, maybe five-six, with delicate, knobby knees and ankles. Pale blond hair covered his legs. Blue veins bulged on his calves. I raised my eyes. He had a masculine face, square chin, broad jaw and a Roman nose. His eyes, though, were long-lashed and baby blue. A cowlick sprouted from his head. His first question was about Michael. I said no, we hadn't found him, and then gestured at the baby. She was a little chunker, with swirls of damp, blond hair plastered to her scalp. Her cheeks were flushed as she sucked ferociously on a giraffe pacifier. "Who's that?"

"Elana . . . my daughter." He sounded embarrassed.

I turned my attention to Matthew, who had left the room long enough to pull on a pair of jeans. He was about my height, with a brown, wavy moptop.

Instantly, I recognized Michael's features in his. Big, saucer eyes the color of Nestle's chocolate. A wide nose, relatively small ears with a funny bump on the lobes. Full lips, with a dimple on the right cheek that didn't require a smile in order for it to make its presence known. He was clearly annoyed. "How did you find us? I didn't give your partner this address and I can't believe Phyl would've betrayed me like this."

"I'm a detective. We have our ways."

He patted the coat pocket where I had deposited my pick. "Did your way include breaking into my place?"

"No."

He shuffled over to Justin, took the little girl into his own arms and told his boyfriend to go put on some clothes. I thought about thanking him, then decided against it. There's something about seeing men in underwear that unnerves me, but these guys didn't need to know that. Matthew looked at me over the baby's head and said, "So why are you here?"

At the moment, I felt pretty damn foolish. Clearly, Michael was not hidden in the bowels of the apartment. I started to apologize for intruding and then stopped myself. Tony had taught me to never assume innocence. "Mind if I check the premises?"

Matthew closed his eyes and raised his chin, as if praying to some deity I personally stopped believing in a long time ago. I didn't wait for an answer. I was halfway down the hallway before he called me back. There was a panicky edge to his voice that made me think he was about to confess. I retraced my steps.

He squished into a leather settee and kissed Elana's downy head. She turned these big, amazed eyes up at him, her chipmunk cheeks dimpling as she pulled hard on the pacifier. After a deep sigh, his eyes fixed on me. "Please don't tell me you suspect me and Justin."

I got to the point. "Is Michael here?"

He made a sound at the back of his throat. "No." He looked disgusted.

"Okay, I'm sure you're telling the truth. Still, I'm a see-for-myself kind of girl. Do you mind?" I pointed down the hallway. He flipped a hand at me with an insolence that made it clear I'd be wasting my time. I didn't let that stop me. There are worse things an insomniac can do than waste time in the middle of the night.

I walked in on Justin just as he finished buttoning his collar. Unlike Matthew, Justin was now fully dressed, in pressed khakis and a starched, white dress shirt. A dry-cleaning bag and two hangers lay on the unmade bed. Except for his bare feet, he looked ready to entertain a client or host cocktails in the Hamptons.

"A robe would have sufficed," I said.

He slid me a sheepish smile. "I had to compensate for the underwear."

"It was nice underwear," I lied.

"You're looking for Michael, aren't you?" He chewed the inside of his cheek nervously.

I gazed past him. The furnishings were fairly traditional. A teak bedroom set, complete with spindle headboard, matching nightstands and a recently polished armoire. I slid open a double closet door for good measure and then said, "Guess he's not here."

His expression turned somber. "I wish he were. That's our dream, you know."

On the night table nearest me was a dog-eared book on incorporating Jewish traditions into the gay lifestyle and a recent copy of *Jewish Monthly*. I had a feeling Justin had a long struggle ahead of him. "What's your dream?" I asked.

"Me, Matt, Elana and Michael. Living as a family."

I had no doubt that a quarter-million could help that dream come true. I pictured the four of them crossing the border in a gray Range Rover, Raffi blasting on the car speakers. Then I wondered how Elana fit in. I asked Justin if his daughter was adopted. He said no and began rifling agitatedly through a sock drawer. If I didn't stop him soon, he'd be putting on a top hat and tails.

"You're married?" My question smacked into his back like a pellet from a BB gun.

He straightened slowly. "Sort of. We're separated."

Uh-oh. "Does she know about your... inclination?"

I watched his shaggy head shake out a negative. "Her family's more conservative than mine, which is hard to imagine. But don't get me wrong... I'll tell Judith eventually, but right now, well... I don't think it'd do anyone good. I mean, things will work out in time. And she's a really good woman. It's not like I don't love her. I do. It's better this way, really, for all of us."

The righteous lie. I'd heard it so many times before. I can't tell my folks, it'll kill them. I can't tell my girlfriend, she'll be so hurt. I can't tell myself, the honesty would annihilate me. I shrugged noncommittally and asked, "What's the reason for the separation?"

He turned around and hopped into his socks. "You mean, what did I tell Judith? I told her I'm going through a life crisis and need time to think things out. Which isn't really a hundred percent untrue, you know. The firm I work for has been going through some hard times ... revenue's down and we've laid off people almost every month. Matter of fact, I've been thinking about changing careers, maybe going into an entirely new field. Medical drawing, maybe. Or investment management." Justin stumbled over his words. The guy was so steeped in his own bullshit, it was tripping him up.

"Are you good with money?"

He hesitated. "I'll probably stick with architecture. After all, it's what I know best." I didn't appreciate his segue. Maybe he was slicker than he appeared.

"How long have you and Matthew been involved?"

A neon smile. "Five months. But this is it for me. No question."

I felt a Mr. Spock eyebrow attack strike. "No question? After five months?"

Surprise twitched across his face. "Yeah. Absolutely. I know it sounds silly, but sometimes it happens that way. You meet someone and boom! All of a sudden, you can't believe you ever settled for anything less. Matthew's just so right for me, a real family man and rock solid. Don't you feel that way about Phyllis?"

Actually, his words made me think of K.T. instead. The realization pissed me off. I didn't have the stamina for reminiscence. "Where were you today, Justin?"

The question hit him while he was bending down to tie his bucks. He carefully rubbed a spot on his shoe with a fingertip moistened by the flick of his pink tongue. "You've got to be kidding." His tone was indignant.

"No. I'm not kidding."

He pulled out of the squat with a little snarl. "I was at a client site in Westchester."

I pulled out my credit-card memo recorder and pressed a button. "Can I have the names of the people you met there?" My eyes watered with the effort to squeeze off a tickle in my nose. Surely any self-respecting kidnapper would confess if only he knew how truly shitty I felt. Unfortunately, Justin didn't tiptoe into my delusion.

"I was alone . . . guess I don't have a good alibi, huh?" He spoke without humor.

"I guess not."

We smiled at each other without congeniality. The tension broke suddenly with a shotgun sneeze that almost took both of us down. I palmed my nose, muttered some dumb nicety and then grabbed a wad of toilet paper from the bathroom right outside the bedroom door. Since I was in there anyway, I figured what the hell and closed the door. I spent a minute spying on the medicine cabinet, one of my top ten predilections. Justin and Matthew had very creative tastes in condoms: triple-ribbed, glow-in-the-dark, pineapple-scented and flags-of-all-nations. Other than that, the medicine cabinet was pretty banal. I shook out a deuce of aspirins then moved out.

I wish I could say I found telltale signs of Michael — the Big Bird bib he had worn this morning at breakfast or his blue elephant booties. But I didn't. The place was clean. I had just entered a room in which Elana lay sleeping when Matthew approached me from behind like a cat with a mouse's tail dangling from its mouth. Except that what he dangled in front of my nose was a cordless phone. I followed him out of the room and took the receiver even though I knew what was coming.

"I can't believe you're *there*," Phyl wailed into my ear.

Suddenly I craved a spot of tea with a swig of rum and honey. "I'm just doing my job, honey." The words sounded heartless, even to my ears.

"I *told* you they couldn't be involved. I know them. Isn't that enough? My God! Can't you listen to me?"

"People aren't always what you expect them to be." I stared hard at Matthew, who stood nearby, close to smirking but smart enough not to go the distance while he was within striking range. I said, "Besides, *even* if they're innocent," stressing the word for Matthew's benefit, "*even* if that's the case, they still may know something that can help me find Michael."

The receiver hissed into my ear. Or maybe it was Phyl. "Well, Sherlock," she snapped, "let me tell you something. While you were out prowling at my ex-husband's, I got another call. He upped the ransom by a hundred grand and now he wants delivery Saturday morning."

I turned my back on Matthew. "When did he call? Was it the same voice?"

Phyl's hubris gave out. The only sound coming at me was her deep, racking sobs.

"I'm coming back now, Phyl. Hang on."

When I faced Matthew again, all trace of petty triumph had evaporated. He wore the face of a frightened parent. "What happened? Is Michael okay?"

I gave him a quick update. "Look," I continued, "I'm sorry for barging in on you and Justin like this, but I do need to talk to you both. For Michael's sake. Can we meet tomorrow morning?"

He sucked in his cheeks. The guy looked ready to hyperventilate. "It's a bad day for both of us. Justin's flying up to Springfield — his dad's going into surgery — and I'm managing this big party at Chelsea Circus. I tried to get someone to cover for me, but I'm the only one not down with the flu. Don't look at me that way." I guess I hadn't covered my amazement too well. "My family's not rich like Phyl's. If I lose this job, I'm screwed big-time, so don't wrinkle your nose up at me unless you know what you're talking about, okay?" He scurried down the hall and rummaged inside a secretary near the front door. "Here's my work number. And here's where I'll be tomorrow night."

I checked out the address. "The community center."

"I run a group for Yeshiva survivors, you know, homos stranded at the crossroads of yarmulkes and rainbow ribbons. It's where I met Justin."

I wondered how he could proceed with life as

usual and if there was a message in his behavior I was missing. Still I cut off my interrogation. Phyl's weary disappointment stung. I had abandoned her for too long and too critical a period and I knew I'd pay for it in the long run. How many relationships have I fucked up because of my impulse to turn tail and run, bury my head in a Sahara of distractions? Maybe I wasn't in love with Phyl. Maybe I didn't know how to play that game. But there was one game I had to fold. If intimacy was going to bite me in the ass, fine. Robin Miller was through playing chicken.

The walnut grandfather's clock in the foyer struck three as I entered. Phyl still somehow managed to look great. Teal stirrup pants were tucked into Italian-made boots and a billowing cream chemise swept past her hips. Her eyes gave her away, though. Bloodshot and hooded, with gray half-circles punctuating her weariness, her eyes fixed on me with equal measures of expectation and distrust.

"They seemed like nice guys," I said, surprised to hear myself voice that assessment of Justin and Matthew. More surprised to realize I meant it.

She shot me a half-smile. "Told you so." The French doors leading into the living room were ajar. She latched onto my hands and led me in, taking small steps backwards. "I really needed you tonight."

I said, "I know," and fought hard against the impulse to dash into the kitchen for an aggressive refrigerator raid. Shit. Maybe I wasn't ready to stop the game. My gaze flitted around the room. Phyl's style was French provincial. Mine is Santa Fe with a touch of Brooklyn. There was only one chair I found really comfortable and that was the rocker near the bay window. I slid into it with a sigh. Every bone in my body ached and swallowing had begun to hurt. This cold was going to be a bitch.

Phyl couldn't decide where to sit. The rocker was nowhere near the formal sitting arrangement she had created by the fireplace which, I noticed with regret, she had not used tonight. Finally she curled up next to me on the floor. I got the message but pretended otherwise. The impulse to change is a lot easier to manage than the deed itself.

I massaged my sinuses and said, "Tell me about the call, Phyl."

The first fact that struck me was the timing of the call, about twenty minutes before my arrival at Justin's apartment building — which meant either man could have made the contact. The second item was how the pick-up for Saturday had been arranged. The ransom had to be placed in the three laundry bags the kidnapper had left behind. Phyl was told to put them in a shopping cart and walk, not drive, to the southwest corner of Union Street and Seventh Avenue promptly at 10:00 a.m. and wait for one of four different public phones to ring. The remaining instructions would be given at that time. The perpetrator was smart. Tony and I couldn't tap those phones without bringing in the authorities, a course of action Phyl had already nixed. And even if we were successful in placing a tap, the kidnapper could bypass that inconvenience by calling the four different numbers, in rapid succession.

"Was the voice mechanized like it was earlier?"

"Mechanized?" Phyl looked puzzled.

"Hon, that wasn't a real voice. Whoever was on the other end was using some device to distort his voice. Matter of fact, we shouldn't even assume it was a man. There's no reason it couldn't be a woman."

Her eyes widened in alarm. "I didn't think about that. The voice. Shit. It *didn't* sound natural." She appeared more agitated about this realization than was warranted. Her words rushed out. "That means whoever took Michael *is* technologically sophisticated, right? Isn't that what it means?"

"Yeah?" I dragged out my response. What was she getting at?

She rested her forehead on my knee and said something to herself. The words sunk into my jeans. I brushed the back of her head and she looked up. "They'll know if you put a tap on my phone. They could have night scopes, cellular intercepts, all kinds of devices. They could be watching us . . . right now."

"Phyl, those devices are awfully expensive." My words were meant to comfort her, but I was having a few problems myself. If the kidnapper was so well informed and organized, why didn't he know I was a private detective? How come he hadn't linked me to Tony? Those questions gnawed at my gut. Something was way off here.

Phyllis rose before me like a cobra, her hands flailing. "What does money mean to these people? Huh? So they spring for a few thousand bucks. The payoff's going to be big, isn't it? Oh, my God. Oh, my God." Her hand clasped over her mouth, her eyes round and frightened, she spun away from me. "What if they hurt Michael? I mean, we really don't know anything about them, do we?" She spoke as if the thought had just fully materialized.

The shock of the day fell from her all at once,

like leaves ripped from a tree by a sudden, torrential downpour, leaving her exposed. I shook my head and joined her in the center of the room. She was shivering uncontrollably.

"We need to sleep, Phyl. Tomorrow's going to be a hard day for both of us."

She nodded, staring through me with unseeing eyes. I led her upstairs, helped her change into a flannel nightgown, laid her on the bed and tucked the blankets around her. She didn't seem to notice or care that I was still in street clothes. I rested on top of the comforter and spooned around her, clutching her small-boned body to me. I wanted her to feel safe, even if the safety was brief and illusionary. For now, that's all she had.

Shortly before dawn, she fell asleep. I untangled myself and shuffled into the bathroom. A few winks hadn't done much to revive me. I stripped, took a hot shower and slunk back into my clothes. Phyl's medicine chest was a little better stocked than Justin's. I downed some nondrowsy Drixoral and more aspirin. My eyes felt crusty and my nose throbbed, but hey, it was a new day.

Unfortunately, the new day started with an old habit. I clanked downstairs, nuked a mug of tea, then headed straight for Phyl's desk in the small den at the rear of the first floor. I don't know what I expected to find, but suspicion is an occupational hazard. I found a check register, which confirmed the Roths' wealth factor. Phyl received a handsome stipend from her parents on a fairly regular basis. Clearly the income she earned as a part-time real estate agent was superfluous. Nevertheless, her spending habits were relatively modest. Upper East

86

Side clothing boutiques, Lower East Side toy stores. No trips to Tiffany's. No fancy restaurants. She drove a 1992 Volvo, a nice car but hardly a showboat. In the few months we had been together, Phyl had traveled three times without me — once to Boston and twice to Amherst, where she and Matthew had lived during their college years. Supposedly, she had stayed with college chums each time. I inspected her credit card receipts, telephone bills and address books. She certainly seemed to have friends in that area and there were no unexpected hotel charges or evidence of sudden debt.

Phyl was clean, which made me feel pretty damn dirty. I never imagined I'd look back on my days as a sleazy, albeit successful romance writer with such nostalgia, but at the moment that was unquestionably the nobler profession.

I didn't let pangs of conscience stop me. Which doesn't say much about my moral caliber, I suppose. Without blinking, I moved on to the file cabinet. The top drawer resisted me. My blood sang. A locked drawer is magical. I don't know how anyone can resist such a siren song. I blew on my fingers for effect and plied my craft. The lock gave with very little ingenuity on my part, which felt horribly anticlimactic. The reward was inside.

Matthew Brickman wasn't kidding when he complained about his financial situation. The divorce had stripped him of all the Roth amenities — condo apartment, car, savings and, of course, Michael. The last factor had clearly been the hardest for him to endure. In letter after letter to Phyllis, he protested the loss of custody. He clearly didn't blame his wife. The true culprits were Oscar and Harriet Roth.

Please, Phyl, you have to make them understand how much Michael means to me. You and I know he will undoubtedly be the only son I'll ever have, at least biologically. This isn't about having someone to care for me in my old age, or any of that shit we used to fight about in the good old bad days. I've always wanted a family. God knows, that's why I married you in the first place, to do the right thing, go the straight and narrow path. I can't do that anymore. For me, the closet is getting way too small and musty. But I want my son with me. You're my only hope. I know your parents hate me. They always have. The son-in-law as loser. But you and I know Mike's better off with me. Don't let them do this to us. I'm begging you. This will break my heart.

The letter was powerful, but apparently not enough. Phyllis had won sole custody. I shuffled through the remaining papers and stopped suddenly when I read my own name on a piece of correspondence dated less than two months ago.

Dear Philly,

Maybe now that you've met Robin, you'll understand what I'm going through. I'm writing you, again, because our phone conversations get heated so fast. I know you're used to lording it over me. That's how we both liked it for so many years. Phyl as butch queen. Matt as gentle clown. But I've blown that suffocating cocoon and I'm determined to fly. This time you have to believe me.

I want Michael to be my full-time son, no more of this "every other weekend" shit. I'm tired of sneaking in visits behind the Grand Master's back. Maybe I was an asshole for telling your father the truth. Maybe you're right on that front, though I still think it probably wouldn't have made much of a difference in the long run. In any case, I refuse to suffer for the rest of my life because I had the balls to come out to one asshole. You know I don't have the money to fight a custody battle with you, and even if I did, I'm not sure I could force you to admit the truth of your life even now.

You pray Robin's the one. Great. I wish you much luck. But I know Justin's the one and I want a life with him and Michael. We all have a lot to work out. You say you're already convinced Robin is not parent material. What if you're right? If you can't think about my happiness, think about yours. My patience is wearing thin. We've gotten this far without extraordinary ugliness. Please, please, don't let your own fears, greed and parental baggage be the trigger that blows us all sky high.

Matt

Sweat trickled down my forehead as I tucked the letter into my back pocket. A broken heart is a mighty effective fuse. I had no doubt the countdown had begun for Matthew. The question was, had the bomb already gone off?

Chapter 5

Thursday morning, almost eight o'clock. Less than
twenty-four hours had passed. I was in my own
well-stocked kitchen, butt on a hard stool, a cool
aqua counter under my elbows, cats mewing at my
heels and a cup of tea snared between my hands. As
far as I'm concerned, tea tastes like soil. Damp, acrid
soil. The only time the damned liquid hits my tongue
is when I'm sick. Just the sight of a Lipton
flow-through can send shivers through me, evoking
decades of sore throats, sinus infections, stomach
viruses and flus. I took a deep gulp and grimaced.

Once I was in San Francisco during a good-sized quake. It was like standing in a rowboat during a bad storm. Taxis around Fisherman's Wharf popped up and down as if they were on Pogo sticks, changing lanes without volition. That's exactly the sensation I had now. My balance was shot. A child's life depended on me and I felt out of control.

I shoved the phone away from me. For the past twenty minutes, I had indulged in something entirely foreign to me. An emergency therapy session. Christ! Even the words made me gag. But I did it. Without provocation, I might add. Called up Vivian and, without filling in the details, painted a pretty clear picture for her. She got it at once. For the second time in my life, a child's life or death rested in my hands. Or at least that's how my stunted psyche sucked it all in. Sure, I'm not three years old anymore, and I don't have my father's twenty-two caliber in my dumb, fumbling fingers. Carol's long dead. And Michael could still be alive. But for how long? And what if I failed? Wouldn't that be like killing my sister all over again?

Vivian wanted me to come in for a full session at two, but I declined. Therapy is a bit like candy corn. A few pieces go down real smooth, but a handful can make you puke. I stopped while I was ahead.

Okay. The case was tapping into my worst demons. Time to move on. I did a quick saltwater gargle, which amused my blue-eyed calico a great deal. Mallomar jumped up near the sink and batted my head each time I spat. Meanwhile, Geeja — the sleek, black-haired reincarnation of Cleopatra or Moby Dick — perched on a stool and stared at me with catly disdain. The kitchen started to feel overcrowded so I moved to the living room side of the counter and hit my answering machine. The first call was from my sister, Barbara. I was sorry I'd missed her. She's a CPA and the call was basically to say, 'bye, speak to you after tax season. Back in September we had decided to make more time for each other. We had kept to our word, talking to each other at least three times a week. In that light, her glib *adios* felt like an assault. I fast-forwarded through her jokes. The next call was from Jill. It came in at seven-fifteen this morning.

"Hey. Are you there? Ah, shit. You must be at Phyl's. Sorry. I'll try you there later on, at a decent hour, unless you get this message first and decide to haul your ass over to the office where Tony and I have been pounding the keyboards for the last hour. We've assembled a pretty good rundown of the Breen kidnapping and need to compare notes."

I rewound the tape, grabbed a few travel packs of tissues and started for the door. It opened before I got there. The whole Morris-Zahavi family walked in. I assumed they'd be at work by now. Beth's face was grim, her perky affect replaced with a solemnity that didn't seem to know how to manage her features. She shot me a grin that had more in common with gas pain than with contentment. Dinah, on the other hand, reminded me of a bowl of Jell-O atop a washing machine on spin cycle. She stood there without moving, Carol gurgling on her back, and yet somehow I got the impression that every muscle in her body was twitching.

"Good morning," I said. "If you're looking for breakfast, sorry, I'm flat out of Twinkies."

I got real smiles this time. I almost answered

them in kind, but then I remembered. I had no reason to smile.

Beth answered me with a voice taxed by lack of sleep. "I called in sick . . . we decided to make this a family day. All for one and one for all. I guess you can't join us." She was never very good at slick.

Dinah stuttered. "What's happening, Rob? Do you know anything about where Michael might be? Any leads?" She continued asking me the same question nine other ways. When she was done, I simply said no. She shook her head in response and said, "I'm waiting outside."

Over the past year Dinah's circuits seemed to be getting awfully short. More temper tantrums, impatient outbursts, sullen silences. Over the same period, my friendship with Beth had accelerated. There are times I think we're both compensating for what increasingly feels like Dinah's withdrawal from our lives. The scary part remains unspoken between us — according to my calendar, the trouble dates back to Carol's entry into our lives.

I picked up my house keys. "Guess she's having a hard time with this."

She flickered an eye at me. "Guess so . . ."

"What is it, Beth?"

"It's just hard to shake this sick feeling. You know, Phyl and I walked into the center together, so I found out about Michael the same time she did. It could've been Carol." She zipped her jacket abruptly. "Listen to me going on . . . I really just wanted to see how you were doing. I heard you come home early this morning. I assume you stayed with Phyl last night?"

A chill rippled through me as I nodded.

"How's she doing?"

I gave her a rundown. As I spoke her gaze flickered over me like a scanner. "When'd you start feeling sick?" she asked.

Damn, she was good. "I'm fine, Beth, really."

She narrowed her eyes. Transferred to cartoons, my friend would have had conflicting thought bubbles drawn over her head: *Robin should get to bed immediately before she runs herself down and gets really sick* versus *Robin is Michael's only hope.* I knew because I had the same bubbles floating above me. It took three seconds of silent communication for us to reach an understanding expressed with simultaneous shrugs.

We walked out together. Dinah waited up the block, limbs akimbo. For some reason, an excerpt from Matthew's letter snapped to mind. *You say you're already convinced Robin is not parent material.* How could Phyl have made that assessment in less than three weeks? What fatal flaw had I exposed? This past summer an acquaintance related a conversation she had overhead between K.T. and her friend Lurlene. K.T. had expressed the same exact conviction. How had she put it? "Robin Miller a parent? When hog meat don't attract flies!" A real Bellflowerism.

Sure, I've never felt particularly compelled to drop a litter myself. But why did everyone around me assume that I was inherently unfit?

Beth broke into my self-absorbed musing. "By the way, Rob, I've been meaning to tell you something for a while."

I braced myself. God, here it comes, I thought.

Why do friends insist on honesty? Personally, I think it's highly overrated.

She squeezed my arm and said, "I'm real proud of you." Her kiss was quick and unexpected. A lump blipped into my throat, which hardly needed another impediment to the basic functions of swallowing and breathing. Still a small smile crept around my lips as I gulped for air like a guppy flopping on a bathmat. Women. Go figure.

Jill kept my spirits up with the delightful greeting she belched at me the minute I entered the office. "It's goddamn midmorning and *now* you show up! All of a sudden the insomniac sleeps in. You shithead. We're in Tony's office." She sashayed away from me.

I checked my watch. It wasn't even nine yet. Not that it mattered. I knew Jill wasn't really mad. She was just being friendly. Her bark meant, great to see you, hope you're okay, now let's get down to business. In the topsy turvy world Jill, Tony and I inhabit, the exchange was akin to a hug.

I got an equally warm reception from Tony. "If you're still sick, move your chair by the window. Open it a crack. And cover your mouth when you cough. There's a full box of tissues on the table. Use them."

The visitor chair had a heavy aluminum frame. No one offered to help me lug it over to the corner. I made it over and collapsed with great sound effects. "Enough with all this small talk and congeniality," I said. "What do you have for me?"

Tony spun around with a squeak of his desk chair. "Got a pad and pen? No? Jill." He thrust a set at her, and she delivered the items into my open palms with the efficiency of a surgical nurse, then exited the room. Tony continued in his best high-cop mode. "The kidnapping took place on September three-zero, at Sterling Child Watch, on Sterling between Sixth and Seventh. Sterling's changed its name, by the way. Can't blame them. New name's Slope Kids. The place is a six-minute walk from Second Home, seven tops. I timed it myself this morning. Parents at both facilities share the same demographics. Some gay, some straight, all middle- to upper-class. We need to get a roster to see if there's been any overlap between the centers. That kid, Olivia Walker, seems pretty clean. When I left here last night, I stopped by her place. She was watching David Letterman and sipping cappuccino. Not tea. I thought the English had tea for blood, but this kid makes a solid cup of joe. We had a long talk. She volunteers for that group, Pet Watchers, for people with AIDS. I don't know. She dresses like a punk, but like they say, you can't always judge people by their looks. She has a pretty strong opinion of Alexander and not much different from my own."

Jill returned with a cup of tea she clacked down on the glass table beside me without ceremony.

"What about me, Jill, huh?" Tony whined. "All *she's* got is a cold. Me, I got AIDS. You should be spoon-feeding me oatmeal with well-cooked raisins."

Jill grunted, which was all the response Tony needed or deserved. He smirked at me. This was more payback for my misguided show of sympathy last night.

My partner smacked his lips. "Let's move on to the Breens. The family's well off." He was back to business, apparently satisfied that his point had nicked my consciousness. "Still, there's no way you could measure their wealth on the same scale as the Roths. Desiree Breen's a contributing editor to some women's magazine. Rusty Breen's a highbrow management consultant, also known as 'Primo Hatchet Man' by the poor suckers whose asses get canned on the basis of his recommendations to the suspenders-and-golf-club set in corporate New York. The only inside word I could drag out of my contacts is that the feds' top suspect was a disgruntled marketing VP from some firm called Open Fields. Apparently Breen was the muscle behind their recent downsizing."

I leaned forward in my seat. "Isn't that the new supermarket chain that's been in all the papers? 'Open Fields . . . because we care about your family as much as you do.' "

Tony looked perplexed, but Jill got it right away. "Sure. There's one out in Metuchen and another just opened near my mother-in-law's house in Montclair. The supermarkets are so politically correct they don't even give out plastic or paper bags. You have to come with your own 'carry device' or buy one of Open Fields' special green-cotton mesh bags. At a premium, of course. Environmental consciousness doesn't come cheap."

Tony scratched his chin and asked, "So why do the two of you look like you know something I don't?"

"The Roths own Oscar's, remember?"

He blew out his cheeks. "Did I know that? Yeah, I guess I did. Okay. So that could be another connection. Or just a coincidence." Jill and I waited while he jotted a note to himself. He dropped his pen, looked up and said, "The discrepancy between Breen's income and Roths' bothered me, but then again the ransom was scaled down as well. One hundred thou versus a quarter mil."

I interrupted him. "Up that by another hundred Gs." I liked the way their attention sprung suddenly to the sick girl languishing in the corner. I blew my nose, then related the details of last night's activities. It took me less than fifteen minutes, including three sneeze breaks and one cough. I'm a great synthesizer.

Jill said, "I take back what I said earlier. You're no slouch."

"Bullshit! She's an idiot," Tony countered. "Since when do you try breaking into an apartment *before* determining occupancy status? You getting sloppy on me, Miller? 'Cause if you are, you know where to find the door."

"Get a new tune, Tony," I said impatiently.

" 'Man who is in honor, and understands not, is like beasts that perish.' Psalms —"

I didn't let him finish the citation, interrupting with a paraphrase of his favorite quote from Job. "Great women aren't always wise."

His jaw line pulsed. "Fine, fine. As long as you know it'll be your ass rotting in a jail cell, not mine." He retrieved a printout from his desktop. "Okay, where was I before the two of you decided to take me down the grocery aisle? Oh, yeah . . . the ransom. The first demand came in over the phone line, just like it did with Phyl. There were a few follow-up contacts, some phone, some paper. We gotta find out exactly what was said and when. One thing we do know. There was no increase in demand with the Breens, which could mean our kidnapper's getting bolder, greedier or just crazier. If that's the case, we could all be lighting candles at mass this Sunday."

"We're Jewish, Tony," Jill said.

Tony waved her comment aside. "So light them at synagogue, what do I care? The feds found no artifacts of any kind . . . no fingerprints, threads, shoe scuffs, spit. Nothing. The pick-up took place three days after the kid was snatched which, I should add, was also a Wednesday. So far, the cases pretty much match pattern. The last call came in at a phone booth, location not specified in the press, and the Breens were sent to make the drop, location also not specified. The backpack contained funny money. Even with a posse of feds and cops, somehow the bastard got to the bag unnoticed and slipped out of the net. Last call the Breens got said, 'Fuck you and your kid.' Then nothing since. The investigation's still active, but nothing's broken for over four months. Oh, one last thing . . . the Breens got proof their kid was alive prior to the drop-off. A videotape deposited on a neighbor's stoop late Friday night. You gotta remember that. Jeezus."

We all fell silent. The picture playing in my head made my jaw clench. At the time of the kidnaping Alice Breen had been twelve, maybe thirteen months old, a chubby baby with wispy strawberry blond hair and big, bright eyes. In the video shown around the clock on every network station, dirt matted her hair and dried food coated her cheeks like a skin disease. She was curled in a laundry basket with the latest issue of *The New York Times* stretched across her. The paper blanketed her entire body, underscoring her size and vulnerability. Her televised cries had been without sound and her eyes without tears. I remembered how one commentator had described the process of dehydration in a dry, emotionless Ken-doll voice. I didn't know what would be worse — receiving a similar video of Michael or never receiving any concrete proof that he was still alive.

Tony cracked the silence with a cough. "There's still a chance that Phyl may get another call, so Jill should move quick on those taps."

I did a quick dab at my drippy nose, then asked if Jill had begun the background check on the families from Second Home.

Jill flipped open a manila folder and handed out photocopies to Tony and me. "Started, but not finished." I stared at a table indicating the names, occupations, addresses and phone numbers for each family contracting with Second Home. The fifth column was headed "MOM" for motive/opportunity/means. Every cell was blank. The final column held a number from one to five. The SIA reason-to-suspect factor. No one ranked higher than one.

"Not very promising," I commented.

"Neither is this case." I turned back to Tony. He crumbled up his copy and hurled it against the wall. "We need more people, more resources. We're in way over our heads." He squinted at me. "I don't know if you appreciate what we're up against."

"Let me guess, Tony. This could be a copycat kidnapping, or the second in a series. We have a dozen suspects, easy, but no hard leads. Phyl's got our hands tied, our lips stapled shut and our options squeezed to nothing like an orange out of juice. Oh, yeah, and Michael could already be dead. Did I leave anything out?" The recitation made me feel feverish.

Jill jumped in. "You and Tony are wasting time

in your silly battle for pessimist points. We can sit here and wring our hands or get this show on the road. Since you two are the esteemed senior partners and I'm just the hired help, you tell me which way we go. I'm waiting." She sat down and crossed her arms, eyebrows raised at us in challenge.

"Listen to her," Tony said, jabbing the air in her direction.

"I am." I stood suddenly. The room did a little spin. So much for drama. I dropped back into my seat and made my spiel. By the time I was done, we had agreed to pull in two more computer researchers, including my friend Roach who has the unsettling habit of referring to his Gateway desktop as his significant other. The guy's been babbling to me about the Internet and how he can gobble up data like a shark sucking in plankton. And I was data-hungry. I wanted financials, credit reports, police records, notices of civil suits, marriage licenses, traffic violations, you name it, for everyone associated with either Second Home or Sterling Child Watch. I doled out assignments like a card deck, then I stomped out of Tony's office and into mine like Rambo on antihistamines.

I did a neck roll, hoisted a hip onto the desktop and dialed Phyllis. She answered on the third ring. Her obvious relief at hearing my voice pinched my conscience. When this crisis was over, we'd have to talk. For now, I pressed a fingertip against my temple and let her whisper into my ear about how much she missed having me in bed when she woke up.

"Same here," I said dully. "Phyl, I'm going to have a jammed day so don't get worried if you don't hear from me until tonight. But I do need your help. I've got to talk to your father —"

"Is that really necessary?"

"I'm afraid it is. For more reasons than I can go into right now. You got to trust me on this."

A sudden intake of air. "He's here, Rob. He showed up about ten minutes ago."

"I'll be right over."

"Uh, Rob?"

"What?"

I hated the pause on the other end. Phyl was working up to something. Finally she said, "You're not wearing the outfit you wore last night, are you? I mean . . ." She lowered her voice. "You looked hot, but my dad doesn't appreciate hot. You know what I mean?"

Unfortunately, I did. "Phyl, I'm not putting on pearls."

She laughed uncomfortably. "Of course not. I'm sure you'll be fine."

After we hung up, I dug in my closet. For an instant, my hand brushed the little black plastic garment bag that contained one of my favorite outfits. I wore it during a search for a runaway who had joined a gang from Kitchen. Tony called it my motorcycle-momma outfit. Wouldn't that be right up Oscar Roth's alley, I thought, a mischievous grin flickering over my lips. In the end, I settled for a staid pants suit. Muted gray tweed. White, button-down shirt. Black pumps. At the last minute, I changed my earrings. Amethyst triangles. It was the least I could do.

Phyl buzzed me in after forcing me to identify myself formally instead of my usual, "Me." She came to the door with her eyes wide in warning. I was being instructed to *behave* and it grated on my nerves. I don't have a hard time lying. I enjoy doing things I'm good at, and subterfuge tops the list. But I hate being forced to lie because it suits someone else's needs rather than mine.

I pointed to the gold chain around her neck. It held a charm I'd never seen before: a scripted *Phyllis* with a diamond dot over the "i" and another sparkling inside the "P." The piece was gaudy and not at all like the woman I had been dating.

She shrugged sheepishly. "It's a gift from my parents. I always wear it when they're around. Come on. They're waiting for you."

Oscar Roth was sprawled, man-style, on the old-fashioned, claw-legged chair I hate most. It wasn't a good sign. His knees jutted in opposite directions, probably because his fat thighs and stomach prohibited him from crossing his legs. There was no apparent excuse, however, for the way his arms hung over the wings of the chair like some tribal chief awaiting delivery of a fresh-roasted pig. I introduced myself politely and extended my hand from a good three feet away. The bastard was going to stand up for me if I had to rent a goddamn crane.

With a grunt and a little sideways rock, he lifted himself up and lumbered over. No question about it. In a previous life, Oscar Roth was a grizzly. Given the frigid temperature outside, I was surprised he had been able to straggle out of hibernation long enough to make the trip in from Long Island.

"You remind me of someone," I said spontaneously.

"Richard Burton, no doubt." He had a booming

103

voice, the kind that could flatten people sitting on the far side of a boardroom with one hot breath.

Finally, the resemblance clicked. He was a Jonathan Winters clone, minus the twinkle in his eyes. I smiled and said, "You're absolutely right," because that's the only answer this man wanted to hear. He snorted and crushed my palm in his sweaty paw. I squeezed back hard, recalling that cold viruses are most efficiently transmitted through hand-to-hand contact.

"Miller. Miller." He toyed with my name like it was a bag of catnip. "Are you Jewish?"

Behind him Phyl winced. I didn't mind the question. The man was getting down to business — at least business the way he saw it — and finding out how he saw things was *my* business.

"Yes, sir. My father was a holocaust survivor. My mother and grandmother had the good sense to move to America two nights before Kristalnacht." For the first time in recent memory, honesty served me better than a pretext.

He nodded solemnly at my credentials. I hoped he didn't ask for details. My family isn't great at details. Probably because they aren't great at communication.

"What camp?" he asked, my hand now pressed between both of his. No doubt about it. We were bonding.

"Sir," I said, extracting my hand carefully. "If you don't mind, I'd rather not discuss this particular matter."

"Of course not. Oscar, leave the poor girl alone. She's a detective, not a new face in synagogue." A slender woman with Phyl's good looks clacked into the room on patent leather high heels. "I'm Harriet, honey. Michael's grandmother." I liked her instantly. She was the kind of rich I could relate to, the kind that fell into it by accident. The money was great, but hey, why change the personality. She wore a simple A-line skirt, a cozy wool cardigan with pills near the armpits and a shimmery Peter Pan collar blouse. From the look of her eyes, I guessed she had probably spent most of the night crying. Her hand was small-boned and her skin rough.

"Have you done this kind of work before?" she asked, almost willing me to say yes.

I reverted to myth. "Only once, ma'am. And we brought the boy home safe."

She frowned, then smiled briefly, her eyes glassy and kind. "I'm sure you'll do your best," she said in a near whisper.

With a zing of astonishment I realized she had seen through my lie immediately.

"Harriet, please." Oscar cleared his throat meaningfully. The man was not about to let the two of us connect. "Go back inside. This is too painful."

"She may be able to help," I said quickly.

He threw me a puzzled look, then realized his faux pas. "My wife's not strong." There was a definite swipe at Phyllis in his remark. "She has a weak constitution . . ."

"Oscar, I'm still in the room. Don't talk about me in the third person."

"Harriet." He dragged out the syllables of her name. "Let me handle this. I've already been in touch with the bank. I know what I'm doing. Phyl, please, take your mother inside. Isn't Regis on?" The last question dripped with condescension.

I started to ask him a question, but he slid me a

wink and held his index finger to his puckered lips, waiting until wife and daughter had disappeared.

"Now," he said dramatically. "Now we talk. Between you and me, I don't mind telling you, you have no business in such a field. But Phyllis insisted. She said the kidnapper...*phui.*" He pretended to spit. "The kidnapper saw your partner...a New York detective, no?"

I nodded quickly.

"Yes. That's what Phyllis said. He saw this man and knew instantly he was a cop. So I thought, maybe my daughter's right for once. A woman, no one would suspect, but a man...yes. And what makes the FBI so special, anyway? I read the papers. That director of theirs is a *schlemiel*...hauling his dog Pete around in an FBI car. Who needs that? You remember the Breen story, no? Such a *shonda*, that was. But what happened then, huh? They tried to get fancy and *nu*? The child's dead. That won't happen to my Michael, I tell you."

It was a direct order. The frightening part was, he sounded like Phyl. Her take-charge personality descended directly from this man. I shuddered.

"That's my goal too. Why don't we both sit?" Now that he had put me in my place, he was ready for the interrogation. I started with a question about Matthew. Wrong move.

"What? Is he behind this, because if that little *faggala* is, I'll pick him up in my bare hands and twist him like a pretzel. Tell me now."

"I doubt it."

He simmered down. "Ah, how could he be? To do this, you need balls. He has no balls. To do this, you need ambition. He has no ambition."

My armpits felt damp. A sweat bead crawled down my spine and still I felt cold. I wasn't sure if it was fever or disgust. Oscar Roth made the kidnapper sound like an enterprising businessman. My sympathies went out to Matthew. If he had master-minded the kidnaping, I'd find out soon enough and deal with him accordingly. But for now, I decided to leave him out of the equation. I shifted subjects. "Do you have any idea who would want to do this to you and your family?"

He pointed a finger. "Again, Matthew." So much for changing topics. "And also my gardener, clerks at the bank. Anyone who knows we have money. Who does that leave out? Children, maybe."

"Do you have any business enemies? Fired employees? Competitors? Disenfranchised partners?"

"Partners? Who needs partners? My business is all me. No one helped me get there. No one. But does anyone appreciate that? Not even my own family."

I pinched the bridge of my nose and squeezed my eyes shut. Maybe if I didn't have to look at him. "Mr. Roth, please answer the question. Can you think of anyone who might have a grudge against you?"

"No." The answer was abrupt, proud and ripe with bullshit.

"I understand that you're a major investor in an upstate lab that experiments —"

"Propaganda! You mean that *New York* magazine filth they wrote about me? Yes, I'm an investor. You'd rather have my grandson's eyes burned out than a rabbit's, huh? You understand the atrocities of the holocaust. Experimentation on people I would never tolerate, but experimentation is essential to progress. New medicines, new products. Where do these come from, I ask you? They must be tested. All those protestors, do they stop using shampoo, headache medicine, athlete's foot powder? No. How would they have us find new products? Voodoo?"

"The lab's been accused of causing excessive and unnecessary harm to animals."

"Yes, this is true." He was in interview mode. I could have been a reporter from Fox News. "And my people are investigating this charge even as we speak. If this is true, I will withdraw my backing at once."

"Has your family received threats of any kind?"

He ticked off a litany of insults, verbal, written and otherwise. Apparently the Roths had suffered their share of hate mail, prank calls and threats, several anti-Semitic in nature and two recent incidents in which red paint had been spilled outside the entrance of Oscar's headquarters in Islip.

One name sprang instantly to mind. Joyce Gass, one of the mothers from Second Home. Oscar Roth shook his head, said he hadn't heard of her or the environmental publications she works for. I paused to read through my notes. So far all this conversation had netted me was a riproaring headache. I started to sneeze and was surprised to find Roth handing me a handkerchief. "You should take care of your cold," he said kindly.

I wiped my eyes first, then my nose.

"Keep it. You need it more than I do. I only needed it for tears. This morning I decided, no more tears. Michael's coming home. If I have to sell Oscar's to bring back my boy, I'll do it. Anything. You do understand?"

I nodded, then said, "But I have to level with you, Mr. Roth. We may lose the money and —"

He flipped his palm up like a traffic guard. "You will not lose the money or my grandson. I'll tell you something I learned on my way up. What you think," he said, stabbing his temples for emphasis, "is what you make happen. Bring home my grandson and my money. If these are your thoughts, they will be your actions."

If only it were that easy, I thought. "Are you familiar with Open Fields?"

"Who could not be? The company's the fastest growing chain in the market."

"The vice president of marketing —"

"Peter Wang?"

"How long has he been with them?"

"I don't know. September, October. Ever since they kicked out Eddie Graves. Why?"

The name plucked a chord, but my ears and instincts were too damned clogged to get the note straight. I said, "There was some speculation that a former employee of Open Fields, a VP of marketing, was involved with the Breen kidnaping."

"Not Eddie. Why would he need to do such a thing? You wouldn't believe the golden parachute that man got."

"You know him personally?"

He shrugged. "I've never shared a Sabbath meal with him, no. But I met him a few times. Trade shows, food conventions. The news was all over the trade papers. He wrote me when he was fired, looking for a job."

"I heard that Rusty Breen had crafted the downsizing at Open Fields. Maybe Graves was looking for revenge."

"Eddie wasn't let go because of the reorganization. There was no need for revenge."

"Did you interview him personally?"

"No. I didn't have to. He's not my kind of people."

I wondered if he meant *not Jewish*. "Can you elaborate?"

"Ah. You think I mean a Jew like us. No. A Jew can't afford such prejudices."

I wondered why his generosity didn't extend to homosexuals.

He waved a hand at me and continued. "No. Eddie's too slick, too hungry, too dark-eyed. A snake. He belongs on Madison Avenue, not in Islip."

"Do you know where he lives?"

"Here, in Brooklyn. He put it in his letter to me, he thought he could schmooze me. 'I live in the same neighborhood as your daughter,' as if I hire employees for such reasons."

That's when it clicked and clicked hard.

Eddie Graves. At Second Home, he had introduced himself to me as Edison Graves. The bastard in the wool coat who had sneered down his nose at me when I complimented his daughter.

It would be a pleasure to take him down.

Chapter 6

Tony wasn't impressed. "The Feds ruled him out. That's good enough for me."

I was hunkered down in Phyl's office, a phone plastered to my ear to drown out the sounds rushing in from the hallway where the Roth family had gathered for battle. I fingered a photograph of Phyllis and Michael and asked, "Were you always such a downer?"

"Only since I got AIDS. Poor me."

"Give it a rest, Tony. I got the point last night."

Our conversation continued in that vein for a few

more minutes. Maybe we both just needed the distraction. When we veered back on track, Tony agreed to build a detailed dossier on Graves. Since legwork's my bailiwick he gave me the home address and number, then informed me that he and Jill had eliminated almost all of the Second Home families from the suspect list.

"Great. What are we down to? Ten suspects?"

"I lost count," he said sarcastically. "We got this guy Graves, who's way down on my scale, the ex-husband and his buddy, that weirdo who lives across the street, what's his name? Elmore Wilmington. Even his name stinks. I'm checking to see if he's got a license for that thirty-eight he's got stashed."

I shifted the phone to the other ear. "What about Karen Alexander and Joyce Gass?"

"I gotta say, I doubt a woman's behind this. Kidnaping for ransom is man-stuff. Women snatch babies for emotional reasons, not money. Trust me on this one."

"Sure. I'll bet Michael's life on the strength of your prejudices. No way, partner."

"Suit yourself. You want to disregard decades of ace detective experience, it's your call. Meanwhile, I got work to do. We'll catch up later."

I replaced the receiver and exited the office. The family was still huddled in the hallway. Oscar Roth had his hands over his ears, the monkey who could hear no evil. Harriet and Phyl conceded whatever point they had been trying to make with matching flicks of their hands. I tapped on the wall and all three turned anxious faces toward me. From now on, when people ask me why the notion of family doesn't exactly ring my bells, I'll point them in the direction of the Roths.

I shouldered through them and dropped my polite veneer long enough to point out that Phyllis owned a very nice-sized duplex, with a living room big enough to fit all of us. To my surprise, they followed me without comment. I spent another twenty minutes covering old ground and comforting the family, then I extricated myself. I said good-bye in the living room, shook hands with a blustering Oscar Roth and let myself out. I hesitated outside, expecting Phyl to steal a private moment with me. When she didn't show, I tunneled into my coat and took off down the block.

Edison Graves lived midway between Second Home and the former Sterling Child Watch. According to Tony, Graves owned a co-op in a four-story refurbished factory. It was the best address on a so-so block, so I wasn't surprised to find a doorman. An Al Pacino look-alike stood outside, leaning on a concrete planter, a cigarette dangling from his bottom lip and a radio pressed to his ear. He wore a jean jacket over a Grateful Dead T-shirt. The front and inner doors were propped open with bricks. The only substances that could make him so oblivious to the cold were drugs or booze. Or just garden-variety stupidity. I banked on the latter, said, "Hey, great T-shirt," and started past him. He jerked himself upright, so I quickly added, "You're not the same guy we had last month, are you?"

He looked at me like he should know what I was talking about. "You mean Manny?"

"Yeah, that's him." I continued to drift through the door. "What happened to him?"

"He's on the night shift now."

"Oh . . . yeah." I slapped my forehead. "How stupid . . . well, have a good day."

In the elevator I considered a persona transformation. A quick search in my Land's End briefcase netted bad news. My favorite business-card assortment pack was back at the office in the leather attaché I had used last night. With a ping of disappointment, I realized there was a good chance I'd have to be me.

With six apartments per floor, finding the one that belonged to Graves was a snap. I rang the buzzer and waited a full minute. There was no answer. I cupped my ear to the door. The drone of a television hummed through the metal. I rang again. I was weighing my options when someone hallooed me from down the hall. A buxom blond bearing a half-empty laundry basket lumbered toward me. She was attractive in a bleary, all-American way. Cool blue eyes, narrow lips, the best nose money could buy. She wore a tight cotton sweater and stirrup pants. A thin line of skin peeked through the joining line. "Can I help you?" she asked, with a healthy dose of suspicion.

To get anything out of this one, I'd have to play my cards carefully. I retrieved my P.I. license and flashed it at her. She stretched her neck and glanced at my paperwork, all the time keeping the laundry basket jammed between our midsections. In the next minute it became clear that she overestimated my authority.

Her lips curled and she rolled her eyes at me. "Shit. Another cop. When is enough enough?" She pressed the laundry basket against the door with her flat stomach and scooped up a set of keys. The door pushed open and the first thing I saw was Kirsten, lying prone in a crib hardly big enough to hold my cats comfortably.

"Is your husband home, Mrs. Graves?" I dragged my attention away from the crib.

A snort accompanied the glance she threw at me. "No. I'm alone, so feel free to pump me. And call me Sara . . . I've met so many of you, by now we should be on a first-name basis, don't you think?" She dropped the basket from hip-height. A pair of underwear popped over the side. "Or maybe I can save you the breath . . . God . . . I know the routine so well already. Yes. Eddie was fired from Open Fields. No, I don't believe he slept with that asshole secretary of his. For one, she's too fat. Eddie likes his women thin. Come with me." She marched down the hall, speaking all the while. "Two, she's Cuban and Eddie's a bigot."

I was surprised at the size of the apartment. In Park Slope, people get away with calling walk-in closets second bedrooms. The Graveses had the real thing. Three bedrooms, each at least ten by twelve. It was a superb piece of real estate and clearly cost a mint. We entered one room at the end of a T-shaped hall that was crowded with exercise equipment, free weights, Nordic Track, stationary bike and assorted torture devices sporting steel frames, hard rubber, thick springs and chains. "This represents about seven years of birthday presents from my husband." Her words were rehearsed and her tone weary. From her affect I began to suspect Edison Graves of having a spectacularly low boiling point. "One hour every day of my life is spent in this room. Here," she said, lifting her blouse and presenting her stomach to me like a cup of coffee. "Feel."

I've never felt a washboard stomach on a woman before. It was like stroking the tire of an eight-wheeler. Personally, I prefer the texture of flesh.

"Now think of Mariela," she said. "Do you think my husband would really risk his job to sleep with someone like that? Get real."

We trooped back into the living room. Kirsten had not moved. I'd never seen a kid so immobile and it scared me. I leaned into the crib, scooped the little girl into my arms and asked, "Is your daughter all right?"

Alarm sprung into her eyes. "What are you doing?" She snatched the baby from me. "You have a cold, don't you? My God!"

My face reddened. "I'm sorry. She just looked so . . ." The word popped out before I could stop it. "Untouched."

She immediately placed the baby back in the crib. "Like you don't know. Christ. What bullshit. You people have been crawling over our lives since September. Kirsten is an AIDS baby, okay? My husband and I had a brief period of experimenting with drugs. It was stupid and we'll live to regret it the rest of our lives. Or at least Edison will. Me, well, we'll have to see, won't we? Excuse me."

In the kitchen, she scrubbed her hands with antibacterial soap and then asked me to do the same. "I've had this horrible stomach flu. Eddie thinks I'm exaggerating, but what's new?"

What a happy marriage, I thought. Made me want to grab Phyl, run down to City Hall and register as domestic partners. I sneezed, blinked to clear my vision and asked, "What can you tell me about what happened at Sterling?"

She handed me a paper towel and groaned. "Ed had nothing to do with that poor girl. Nothing. Believe me, we were as shocked and as horrified as any other family. Why do you think we moved Kirsten to Second Home? Because we wanted to spend more money for child-care? I don't think so. With Ed unemployed... look, I'm not saying that I don't make enough as a hand model to offset the cost of child-care — I do — though I suppose we'd be better off if Ed took care of Kirsten. But looking for a job in New York is full-time work and, honestly, Kirsten's probably better off with Karen Alexander than with either me or Ed."

On that point I readily agreed. "I understand you're having some financial problems." Actually, I didn't understand anything, but I was willing to guess.

She opened the refrigerator. I've never seen so much Gatorade and juice in my life. She proffered a bottle of carrot juice at me. I took it with a justifiable degree of trepidation. The stuff tasted like something concocted as part of a kindergarten class project — paste, shredded cardboard, food coloring and a touch of lime. Using all my will power, I managed to swallow instead of spit. Meanwhile Sara Graves gulped the shit like it was a McDonald's milk shake, an item I fully intended to buy as soon as I escaped this den of tragedy and dysfunction.

Sara Graves used the back of her hand to erase a pulpy, orange mustache. She lifted up the lid of a blue recycling pail and spiked the empty bottle. "Why don't you tell me about our financial problems?

117

Aren't you guys the experts by now? Eddie hasn't gambled in over a year. Sure, we're eating through our savings like maggots and on real luxuries mind you, stuff like food, medicine and mortgage bills. Maybe, just maybe, if you people weren't hounding us my husband would be able to find a job a little faster, but I guess that's asking too much."

I followed her back into the living room. "Do you know where your husband is today, Mrs. Graves . . . Sara?"

We stood on either side of the crib. She gazed down at her daughter with an unsettling blend of affection and disinterest. "I wonder, sometimes, if she'll even make it to a year," she mused quietly. "Worse, I wonder if it makes a difference."

The apartment had a bank of windows facing south. Cold, insistent sunlight poured into the room. Radiators hissed like cobras. I zipped the coat I had never bothered to remove, fearing I'd never be able to counter the chill in my bones. "Where can I find your husband?"

The look she slipped me held a modicum of contrition. "He's not off snatching babies, I can tell you that much."

Cognizance sunk in. She had no idea where her husband might be. "Tell him to call me." I flipped her a card and got out of there before risking further exposure to the real disease plaguing the Graves household: emotional malaise.

The slap of frigid air was a sharp release. I decided to skip the milk shake at McDonald's and settled for a mochaccino at Ozzie's, a coffeehouse about two blocks from Second Home. I made it last a long time. I crunched into a chocolate-covered biscotti, undipped, and scanned the newspaper. It wasn't much of a distraction. A serial killer was loose in New Orleans. Here, in my own backyard, a woman had been forced into her apartment and raped at gunpoint. The good news was that graffiti had been eradicated from almost all New York City subway cars.

I let myself have one good, arm-stretching, eye-watering yawn, then I braved the real world again. I wasted the next hour trying to finish my canvass from the night before. Out of fifteen apartments, I got answers at four. I wasn't any closer to finding the kidnapper, but I was doing one hell of a job unearthing those dangerous illegal aliens everyone in Washington was so worried about. Maybe Tony and I were missing out on a lucrative niche.

I rang the final doorbell on my agenda. By then I didn't expect an answer. I gave up after two tries. On my way out I glanced over to Wilmington's place. To my surprise he was sitting on his stoop, burrowed in an army-green parka complete with fur collar. With eyes shut tight and his black hair sprouting from his head like sprigs of rosemary, he balanced a set of bongo drums between his knees. He wasn't so much playing them as he was slapping at them with rapid, sporadic hits. I took a step back toward the garden apartment I had just left and watched his antics. The man was clearly crazy.

"Hey, you! You don't live here."

I looked around. It was Eagle Nose, the mailman I had nearly capsized yesterday. He swung through the gate and pointed a spear of rolled-up magazines at me.

"Hey, you're right." My tone was sarcastic. He

flinched as I stepped toward him, as if he expected me to barrel into him again like a defensive back. Not that I didn't want to. I could've used the release. But it struck me all at once that a mailman could be a great resource. I flashed my most insincere smile and said, "I was just watching that guy over there."

He followed the set of my chin. "Wilmington?"

"You know him?"

"Why you asking?" The guy deflected my gaze by marching around me and spiking a wad of mail into the gated alcove of the garden apartment. The papers fell with a *thwack*.

"Someone's been burglarizing apartments around here. They hit Second Home yesterday. Last week, it was two places on Sterling, including that other day-care center. What's it called?"

"Child Watch." His focus pinpointed on my mouth. The guy was immediately suspicious. "Funny . . . I didn't hear about none of this. People usually let me know when stuff's going down around the nabe, ask me to keep an eye out. I guess they think one G-man's as good as another. Or as bad." He laughed at his own joke, which I didn't quite get.

"Well, whoever's doing this hasn't taken anything of real value." I glanced at Wilmington's stoop and improvised. "Clothing. Musical instruments. Camera equipment."

"Way I see it, people around here think their garbage can's got real value. My brother's in the storage biz. Owns one of the big ones in Jersey . . . you got it, we lock it. He's seen yups pay big bucks to store all kinds of shit — broken chairs, mattresses with their springs popping out." He scratched his neck with a gesture that instantly recalled a PBS documentary on orangutans. "So what's ya name, hon, you from around here?"

I can take "hon" from people in their sixties, but this jerk had less than five years on me. His "hon" smacked of a bar pick-up and plucked my nerves in a big way. I blew my nose in his direction.

"You're not from this block, or I'd know you." He sucked air through the corner of his mouth with a sound that reminded me of a rat's squeak. I gave him the only business card I had. The real one. He read it and clucked his tongue. "Private eye, huh? So, someone's hired you to find their bongo drums, huh, or maybe their stinky Reeboks . . . is that what you're saying? 'Cause if you are, I'd say, go peddle it on Seventh Avenue. Maybe you can find some dumb, old SS recipient who'll buy that line. Whatcha really after? Some broad's cheating husband? An insurance jerk-off? What? Is Robin Miller even your real name?"

My patience crashed. "Why don't you tell me *your* name."

"I'm government issue, babe, I don't have to answer to you."

I sighed, turned around and waved a hand behind me. This guy wasn't worth my time.

"Hey, Nancy Drew, tell me the truth. This about the kidnapping?"

His words yanked the yoke around my neck. I walked back to him. "How do you know about the kidnapping?"

"Who don't know? Do I look like an idiot to you, like I don't know what a TV is? I seen the stories. Christ, for weeks that's all you heard, Breen this, Breen that. Send money to help the Breens. Call one-eight-hundred Breen. I wasn't in fuckin' Alaska.

121

It got so bad, I swear Desi Breen had more air time than Joan Lunden."

The electric jolt eased up. "Do you know the Breens?"

"They're on my route. Why you asking?"

"How well do you know them?"

He shrugged defensively. "Not too. I see them. That's all. Not lately, though. The family's in Ireland visiting relatives . . . stopped delivery for a mont'. Now your turn. Why you asking?"

I bit off the clip and threw my next lie onto the field. "I'm doing some work for them."

"You doing work for them." As he spoke he popped his head back and forth like a turkey on amphetamines. His tone was incredulous. "You doing work for them. What you gonna do that the G's couldn't? You some kind of miracle worker? The kid's gone. Why don't you all leave the family alone." He leaned on the handle of the mail cart so that the front wheel lifted, then let it crash back to the ground. "You know what I think?" He pronounced the word "tink." I waited for his revelation. "I tink you wanna be a hero."

"What's wrong with that? Maybe Alice Breen is still alive."

"And maybe she's not. Besides, what can you do that the cops can't?"

I smiled hard at him. "Plenty."

He picked up a magazine and fanned its pages at me. "Yeah, well, good luck. I'll look for your puss on the cover of the *News*."

"Were you around the day Alice was taken?"

I watched his Adam's apple bob around a bit. "Wish I had been, but I was home sick. Stomach bug. Otherwise, man, that never woulda happened. Not on my route." His machismo made my skin crawl. I said, "Thanks for your help," and asked for his name a second time.

"You want my name? I'll give you my name. Lloyd John DiNardo, Junior. Write it down, babe. It's not a name you're gonna wanna forget."

I stomped away. The gate closed behind me with a metallic clank. Wilmington started at the sound. He turned in my direction, saw me and waved.

"So you know him, huh?" DiNardo exhaled down my neck.

"Not exactly."

He squinted at Wilmington. "The guy moved here a couple of weeks ago, way after Alice Breen was snatched, so why you interested in him?" He scratched his chin. "Maybe the two of you are working some angle."

"Look at him," I said. Wilmington was talking to himself, pounding the bongos, oblivious to the cold. "You think I'm collaborating with someone like that?"

He snorted. "You're some detective. The guy's got that disease, what do you call it? Toored's something or other."

"Tourette's Syndrome?" I first learned about the disease from an episode of "L.A. Law." Tourette's a neurological disorder characterized by facial tics and compulsive outbursts of curses and grunts. I stared toward Wilmington, feeling like an asshole and asked, "Are you sure?"

Eagle Nose read the downshift in my mood. He let out a deep chuckle. "Yeah. He told me himself, just a few days after he moved in. I got real pissed at him for calling me a sodomite cocksucker. I almost fisted him in the mouth ... till he starts yelling at me about how he's got this disease that makes him say shit like that. The only reason I didn't go ahead and sock him in the kisser is 'cause I'd delivered some newsletter to him about it." He stopped suddenly and retrieved my business card from his shirt pocket. I watched him read it again, flicking the edge with a dirty fingernail, his skin turning scarlet. "Unless he's bullshitting me and this disease's just a cover. Maybe you two got some kind of, what d'ya call it, surveillance going on this block."

DiNardo's voice was starting to make my head hurt. I said, "Yeah, we're working for the government, identifying postal workers who spend too much time talking and not enough delivering mail."

He cocked his head at me in a gesture that said, "Get outta my face," in classic Brooklyn fashion. I ignored him and crossed over to Wilmington. Now that I knew he had Tourette's, last night's behavior made sense. But I wasn't ready to write him off just yet. After all, he did have a night scope screwed onto his camera. And the thirty-eight. I waited until he finished a riff, then said hello. He ran a hand through his hair and smiled. A snowflake caught on his eyebrow and both of us turned surprised eyes toward the sky. Fifteen minutes ago the sky was clear. Now it was an opaque gray and a light snow was falling.

I made some dumb comment about the weather and he chimed in eagerly. Wilmington was evidently anxious to talk. I got the impression he didn't have many outlets besides his art and music. We chatted about Michael Jackson, Janet Reno, Rodney King and ended back on the weather. My feet were numb and I was almost out of tissues, so I decided it was time to slide up to home plate. With a bow of my head that was half-contrition and half-artifice, I confessed to my little indiscretion of the night before.

He laughed. "So you snooped around in my treasure chest. You're a lawyer . . . I wouldn't expect less than that." For a second I had no idea what he was talking about and then I remembered. The law profession had been my ticket in the door last night. Wilmington caught a flake on his tongue and said, "I do a little bit of that stuff myself sometimes. Just for fun. Bulldagger! Cunt!" His head twitched three or four times and then he stamped his foot so hard I stepped back. All the while, his gaze remained fixed on me. A little dance went on in his eyes. After a moment he looked past me to where DiNardo was making his next mail drop. "Nardy told you about me, huh? Like he's one to talk about weirdos. No problem. It's better than your thinking I'm some kind of nut like most people do. So what do you want to know? Are men with Tourette's better lovers? Absolutely true. Is there anything wrong with my heart, mind or soul? Only if you have problems with sensitive, passionate men."

The bulb flickered on in my dull brain. Wilmington was flirting with me. I sat down on the stoop next to him and stared out at the street. The concrete was cold and damp and the wind had picked up. I tucked my jacket under my butt and asked straight out, "What's the night scope for?"

"I'm insulted." He paused for a fiery bongo

interlude, complete with foot stomping and bizarre neck rolls. I realized then that the frenetic bongo-smacking substituted for yet another series of explosive tics. I had to hand it to him: the guy was pretty ingenious. He stopped suddenly and shot me a sheepish grin. "Didn't you notice my photographs last night?"

I called up a mental picture of his apartment and drew a blank.

"In the living room. My *Owls in Silver Silence* series. I go up to Prospect Park at night and shoot the owls with slow film. The pictures are really mysterious. Ass kisser! Sorry you didn't appreciate them."

"Oh, I did," I said hastily. "I just didn't realize they were yours."

"Wilmington originals. What did you think? I'm not some type of pervert." He spoke without resentment. "The Tourette's is a disease of the body, not of the mind. My art's going to be worth a lot of money one day. Play your cards right and maybe, maybe, you'll end up owning one."

A shiver racked my body. I stood up and took a good thirty seconds to swallow. My tonsils felt like spiked golf balls. "What about the gun?"

His smile was charming. "Tell me, would you hike around Prospect Park at night without a gun? It's licensed and I'm a pretty good mark when I'm not twitching." He laughed at his own joke. "When I was a young buck I temped as a security guard, but then the Tourette's got less, let's say, controllable."

His explanation was plausible enough. And if he was conning me, I'd know as soon as Tony completed the background check he was running on Wilmington.

After quizzing him on where he used to live, how he got along with his old neighbors and why he moved, I decided enough was enough. I said, "Well, I better be going."

"Want to come inside for some coffee?"

"No, thanks, I've got a long day ahead of me."

"You're lying about being a lawyer, aren't you?"

My stomach lurched. I turned to him and said, "What are you talking about?"

"I made some calls. No one's been scamming people on this block. You made that up. But I won't hold that against you. Lying is just another form of fiction, so I'll just think of you as an artist. But if you ever decided to level with me, come on by. Maybe I could help you out."

I thanked him for the offer, picked up my briefcase and made a beeline across the street. DiNardo was standing outside Second Home when I got there.

"What do you make of that?" He pointed to the front door.

Second Home will be closed the remainder of this week due to a sudden illness in the Alexander family. Arrangements have been made with Slope Kids and Ninth Street MotherWise to accept additional drop-offs. We apologize for any inconvenience this causes in your work schedule.

I cocked my head with surprise. Where the hell was Karen Alexander?

* * * * *

Sometimes I know the right thing to do and do the wrong thing anyway. My cold had started to feel like the flu and I no longer doubted that I had a fever. The right thing to do was to ignore Phyl, call the feds and spend the remainder of the day in bed sipping tea, nibbling white toast and surfing the boob tube. Instead I hung around Second Home for a while, waiting for someone to show. When no one did, I slogged up to Seventh Avenue and grabbed two slices of pizza. I could barely swallow the melted mozzarella, but instead of stopping I just took smaller bites and chased them with hefty swigs of fizzy Pepsi. Afterwards I stopped by the two other child-care centers. No one knew anything more about Alexander's sudden disappearance than I did. By the time I made my way to Phyl's brownstone my eyelashes were iced and my lips cracked from the cold, brisk wind. I rang the buzzer repeatedly. My brain refused to register her absence. I huddled in her doorway, blinking to clear my eyes. Clearly I was too sick to go back into the office. And I needed warmer clothes. After another minute I gave in and headed home. In less than four blocks I lost sensation in my legs. I slapped them until they tingled and kept doing that until I turned onto my street.

Back home I found a note my housemates had hastily shoved into my mailbox.

Phyl called and asked us to keep her company today. She said she was going nuts sitting around and waiting. I guess all of us could use the distraction. Our plan is to take a walk in the park and then have dinner at Santa Fe

around six, six-thirty. Please join us if you can.
(Truth is, no one expects you to show.) We love
you and wish you success. Just don't forget to
take care of yourself.
Love, Beth, Dinah and Carol.

Beth had marked down the time. According to my watch, I had missed them by less than twenty minutes. I started to extract the rest of my mail when all of a sudden my stomach turned. I dropped the note and rushed through the front door in time to toss my cookies in royal style. I hugged the toilet for a solid half-hour. Curled up there between the john and the litter box, I realized any further contact with Tony had to be relegated to phone lines only. For now, the office was strictly off limits.

My stomach finally stopped heaving and I rolled myself into the shower. Afterwards I changed into thermals, jeans, a flannel shirt and a heavy Irish wool sweater. I even donned a second pair of socks. Four aspirins and a cup of tea later I was on a telephone conference call with my office. My head pounded and Tony's voice sounded amplified to rock-concert levels. I leaned my forehead against my palm and tried to focus on the conversation.

Around eleven in the morning Jill had linked a Caller ID deck and a phone tap onto Phyl's line. As far as they knew, the only new call had come in from Phyl's friend in Amherst. No surprises there. The rest of the day Jill and Tony had spent accumulating background data on our pack of suspects. With the help of our freelancers, they had already checked police records and analyzed basic financials on everyone except Karen Alexander. Her name simply had not shown up on any search. Tony asked me for her husband's full name. I muttered something in my defense but the truth was I had dropped the ball. I didn't even know if Alexander was her maiden or her married name. Before Tony could chide me for my poor investigative skills, I put him and Jill on hold and dialed Phyl. I connected with her answering machine. I stabbed the flash button irritably, dialed information and then called Alexander's assistant Olivia Walker. The phone rang seven times. This time I didn't even get an answering machine. I switched back to the office and gave them the news.

"Never mind that," Tony said. "I got a different concern. And it's a big one."

Tony had done more research into the Breen kidnapping. Whoever had called the Breens with the ransom demand had not employed a voice-altering device. Moreover, within twelve hours of the kidnapping the Breens had received a threatening note using words sliced and pasted from a recent issue of *TV Guide*. So far, no similar note had been dropped off at Phyl's. "The more I look at this, the more I doubt it's the same perp," Tony explained. "And if it's a copycat case, the odds are stacked high against Edison Graves being our man. Besides, why would he put his neck out there when the feds are just aching to drop the ax on him? It doesn't make sense."

I joined in. "The mechanized voice makes more sense if Phyl knows the kidnapper."

"Exactly," Tony said. "So I say the perp's a familiar. Like maybe her ex."

"Or Karen Alexander," Jill interjected

"I don't like the woman, but I don't see her in

this thing," Tony said. "Think about it. She obviously didn't make the ransom call and if she's got some unknown cohort working with her, why bother with the mechanized voice?"

"The cohort could be her husband," Jill said. "But let's back up . . . something else bothers me. This kidnapper's pretty damn sharp. So why didn't he know Phyl was dating a private eye? Makes me think it *is* a stranger."

Jill was picking at a sore spot that had been bothering me since the start.

Tony disagreed. "Not necessarily, Jill." I could practically hear him shaking his head. "The kidnapper's sharp, but he's not clairvoyant. What's obvious to you or me could've been easily misinterpreted by someone else. After all, it's not like Phyl's real out there. Maybe the kidnapper just pegged Robin as Phyl's best friend. Or maybe he knows Miller's a neophyte."

I ignored the dig and said, "Best friends don't spend every other night together. Not at our age."

"Rob, I'm telling you that unless the perp's gay himself, he wouldn't necessarily jump to the conclusion that you and Phyl are a couple. Especially not the way Phyl looks. And if he tagged you as a friend, he could've decided you weren't worth backgrounding. Lesson number one, ladies, most criminals are dumber than dirt."

"Well, Tony, based on what you're saying, we can rule out Matthew and Justin."

He rapidly backtracked. "Hey, I'm just playing devil's advocate here. It's way too soon for us to nail ourselves into any box. You want my real opinion? I think whoever did this knows all about you and doesn't see you as a threat. I wasn't just pulling your chain when I called you a neophyte. The truth is, Rob, you're way out of your league on this. I wouldn't be surprised if the kidnapper banked on Phyllis's turning to you instead of the feds."

I bit my tongue and put them on the speaker phone. While the two of them continued to argue the point, I rummaged in my desk for throat lozenges. I found a handful from last winter. They had begun a slow dissolve. I used a fingernail to scrape off the paper wrapping. I popped the green slimeball into my mouth and recoiled from the medicinal taste. Why can't throat drops taste like hot fudge? I spit the lozenge out, then interrupted them. "Bottom line, Jill, and I hate to say this, Tony's right. We don't know enough yet to make any conclusions."

"So where do we go from here?" she asked, clearly frustrated.

In the distance I heard Tony spew one of his dumb aphorisms. I disregarded him and said, "Keep trying Olivia Walker. Maybe she knows where we can find Alexander."

"Done. Anything else?" She sounded worn out.

"You okay?" They both responded at once with competing whines. "Forget I asked," I said. "Jill, there is something else. Can you make it to the gay community center tonight to follow up with Matthew Brickman?"

She hesitated. "John's opening is tonight. I'd really like to be there..." Jill's husband is a professional photographer. This was only his second show in four years. I told her I'd handle it.

Tony guffawed in my ear. "Don't think I'd blend in with the homosexuals, Miller?"

"Go to hell, Tony." My retort only made him laugh harder.

Jill cut in. "I can do it, Rob. Really. You sound like hell."

"Hell would be an improvement, but if you think I'm going to cause friction between you and your sugar poop, you're nuts. Go to the opening. The community center is mine. Tony, can you focus on Graves and Wilmington?"

"Sure, but if you're seeing Matthew tonight, you're on the fox's track. I'm just chasing geese."

"Then chase geese, Tony, you're so good at it." I peeked at my watch. Shit. I had to be at the center in just over an hour. "I'm signing off, boys and girls."

I hung up and for an instant rested my head on my forearms. My spine was stiff, my joints ached and my eyelids felt weighted down by sand bags. Thirty minutes later I jerked awake. I spun toward the door. Something had startled me. I shoved myself away from the desk groggily. My black cat, Geeja, had planted herself on my lap. I patted her butt and she leapt to the floor with a mew of protest. My other cat was curled on the desktop. She raised sleepy eyes and gave me a gravelly, smoker's meow. Whatever had disturbed me had not been cat-produced, nor had it startled them. Still I felt suddenly alert. I lifted a steel paper punch from the desk and hefted it like a club. I edged through my apartment slowly.

Nothing appeared out of place, yet my nerves stayed on maximum burn. The cats met me in the kitchen, howling at me with tails at full mast. I reassured them I was fine, then dished out a full can of people tuna into their bowls. With my girls chowing down, I popped more aspirin then leaned over the sink and splashed cold water on my face. It didn't help much.

I dug around the bottom of my coat closet looking for a scarf and ski gloves. I found both items in a dark corner, dotted with dust bunnies and cat hair. I shook the scarf off and wrapped it around my neck. I hadn't even stepped outside and already I was shaking. The cold had burrowed into my bones and nothing but time was going to make me feel warm. It was just after seven. I locked the door and slipped on my gloves. A full moon rose over the rooftops. Fine white powder coated the sidewalks and the air was still; silver flakes fell in slow motion. I took one small step and went down hard. I cursed and grabbed the bannister. Someone had left a goddamn flyer on my doorstep. I picked it up and shook off the snow.

Back off or Carol's next!

The letters had been clipped from *TV Guide*. The kidnapper had found me.

Chapter 7

I circled onto Thirteenth Street for the fourth time. Parking in Greenwich Village is a little like mining for gold. You have to be sharp, territorial and occasionally vicious. Near the far corner a pair of ruby-red tail lights flashed on. I zipped down the block, cutting off a cab and a Mercedes–Benz.

The heat was on high, the inside of my car a mini-sauna and still I shuddered. I cupped my hands over a vent and watched a bald New Jersey commuter try to shimmy his Caddy out of a tight parking spot without bouncing bumpers. I thought again of the kidnapper's threat and fought back a wave of nausea. I closed my eyes and tried to picture the slushy footprints left behind on my steps. One thing was clear. I had missed the kidnapper or his messenger by minutes. By the time I had retreated inside, contacted Tony and exited for the second time, the prints had been completely eradicated.

Something about the footprints had disturbed me. I bounced my head against the headrest and suddenly my vision cleared. There had been two sets. Two sets. Grateful that Tony had agreed to wait at my place until Beth and Dinah returned home, I pulled away from the curb. I wanted my housemates out of harm's way, and fast. If something happened to Carol —

My mind veered into dangerous territory. I punched the horn. To be fair, the bald Jersey guy was doing his best, but I needed to get out, get moving. He flipped me the finger and purposely slowed his exit. Urban warfare. I played the steering wheel until he finally pulled out and then I banged my way in. I hooked on The Club, slammed out of the car and activated the alarm with an anemic beep. The air smelled of Thai spices from a nearby restaurant. I took a deep breath and ended up in a coughing fit. The cold didn't help. The streets were slick and icy. Snowflakes sparkled in the glare of streetlights but melted before they hit the ground. I had on leather running sneakers, not the smartest choice given the weather. I hit a patch of ice and slid across the sidewalk. I caught myself on the brick face of the Gay and Lesbian Community Services Center.

The building still had the look and feel of a

public school, which it had been in a former life. I took in the harsh fluorescent lighting, institutional pale gray walls with spots of crumbling plaster and tiled floors that amplified the click of heels and the thump of hard rubber soles. The hallway leading to the staircase was lined with metal folding chairs and bulletin boards pinned with advertisements for everything from S&M Sundays to cooking Chinese, lesbian-style. Despite the decor, the aura was high energy — the electric zip of people connecting, closet doors crashing, hormones percolating. Singles of both sexes pranced around like race horses rushing the gates. I walked through the battered front door, glimpsed a male couple making out by the rainbow flag and, for the first time all day, I felt warm.

The announcement board indicated that Yeshiva Survivors met in the Wilde Room on the third floor. I hardly needed the trek, but I slogged up the stairs anyway. I put my ear to the door first. Sure enough, the meeting was already in progress. I sidled through the door quietly. One peek and somehow I knew that I was in the wrong place. Maybe it was the well-dressed woman standing dead center with a speculum in her right hand and a small vial in the left, or maybe it was the stack of photocopies on the table near the door depicting strings of mucus stretched between a thumb and index finger. In any case, I got it right away. I started edging out when a voice stabbed me in the back.

For a moment I stopped breathing. I feared my bowels would explode or, at the very least, my lungs collapse. I was afraid to move. The voice continued to torment. I had to turn around, but one hand remained frozen on the doorknob and one on the wall. My feet had a mind of their own and their mind would not let me retreat.

I tried to locate the voice in the room, but the speculum lady in the business suit and running sneakers intervened too soon. She pivoted toward me and scowled. "Can I help you?"

I swallowed hard, said, "No thanks," and retreated like a chastised pup. I dropped onto the muddy top step, suddenly exhausted beyond measure and used the back of my sleeve to wipe away the sweat trickling down my forehead. Behind me the door opened. Please, God, I prayed. Don't let it be her. Not now. Not like this.

"Robin? My God, it *is* you."

I pinched the bridge of my nose. Tears rose briefly. I pressed them away. With grinding slowness, I raised my eyes to where she stood. Because fate is unkind and mischievous, she looked her astounding best. I propelled myself to my feet and wheezed, "K.T. It's good to see you." My hands clung to the wall. I wanted to pass out. Blood rushed to my extremities. The trembling returned with a vengeance.

Her hand began a languid journey toward me, stopped, reversed directions and ended up squeezed deep into her jeans pocket. The pants were tight, emphasizing the curve of her well-shaped hips and butt. I stared at her and wanted to scream. She was excruciatingly beautiful — her eyes the color of leaves in early spring, her coppery hair cut short, the loose curls framing a face that radiated its own light. And her smile, so delicate, so unsure, took away what little breath I had left. How had I let myself drive her away?

She frowned and said, "You look like shit."

I didn't argue. The last time I checked out a mirror, my nose had that just-scrubbed-with-Brillo glow. I said, "Wish I could say the same to you."

Amusement played in her eyes. "Do I dare ask how you've been?"

I shrugged and blew my nose. The eruption echoed down the stairwell. "What group is that?" I gestured behind her.

She glanced back. "Uh . . . well . . . here goes, I guess . . . it's for women interested in A.I."

A.I. Artificial insemination. Semen to go. Turkey basters. Baby-making. My gaze dropped to her belly instantly. "Are you pregnant?" I could feel my ears starting to burn.

Both of her hands were pocketed now. She rocked onto the balls of her feet and said, "Not yet."

The moment trapped me. I was a fly stupid enough to fumble onto a sticky strip and I had no idea how I was going to escape. On the wall just beyond K.T. I noticed a poster announcing a seminar on gynophobia. Suddenly the subject fascinated me. I moved over and scrutinized the announcement, thinking, K.T.'s going to have a family. My internal censor must have malfunctioned because the next thing I said was, "I guess you're with someone new," which was the last thing I wanted to know. My gaze dropped to the floor. I needed new footwear. Socks too. I'd have to stop at Herman's.

Somewhere out in distant space K.T.'s voice went low and tender. She said, "No, Robin, I'm not," and took a step in my direction. "And you?"

Despite my stuffy head, I caught a whiff of her aroma. After a day at the restaurant she owned, she often smelled like this — fresh baked bread ripe with rosemary and thyme. I dared to glance up. She looked apprehensive. I knew I had to answer honestly, but she was so close and I wanted her so much. I gave her the Cliff Notes version and said, "It's not serious."

It was her turn to look away. "Is it ever?"

Her question knocked me back in time. I remembered making love with her, watching her scamper around the restaurant she owned, gesturing like a maestro, laughing with delight as she fetched me spoonfuls of gravy, fistfuls of snap peas. I remembered waking with her, a lump in my throat as I snuggled against her tightly, amazed at how well I slept with her. Stunned to realize I had not had a good night's sleep since. The instinct to flee, to retreat, was powerful. This woman held domain over me in a way no one else ever had. She terrified me.

I tripped over the hurt in her eyes. "It was with you, K.T."

Her smile was fleeting. "I wish I could believe that, Robin. I really do."

I surprised myself by saying, "Give me a chance to convince you."

She gave a little snort. "I can't believe you." She spoke to a spot over my shoulder. "You stumble into me by chance, *by chance*, and expect me to believe you've been pining over me for months. Come on, Robin. I'm a big girl. You're with someone new. That's fine. Life moves on . . . which reminds me." In slow motion she headed for the door.

I cut her off. "Goddamn it, K.T. Okay, I'm an asshole. I don't know what happened this summer. I fucked up big time. And you're right, I didn't search you out. I'm too much of a chicken. God . . . when I remember the last time we spoke . . ."

"When you confessed to sleeping with another woman?" Her hand hooked onto her hip.

"It was a mistake."

"Sleeping with her or telling me?"

I looked away and felt my cheeks pucker.

"Right," she said. "I thought so."

"No, you're wrong. I'm not playing a game —"

"Isn't your girlfriend waiting for you, Robin? You shouldn't stay away so long, it's dangerous."

My right eye twitched. "K.T., it wasn't all my fault —"

"You blame *me* for what happened?" She jabbed her chest, her eyes wide with disbelief. "You have no idea what I felt like, skunking around with Lurlene, afraid to trust you, afraid to call —"

I broke in. "Trust. How about that word? Let's talk about trust. *You* skipped out on me, remember? Disappeared without a word. I was worried sick about you."

"So sick you had to screw the first woman you met, right? Poor baby. How could I have been so uncompromising? After all, you just needed to allay your tension. Shit, Robin, don't you think it's time to 'fess up?"

"That's not what I'm saying . . . Damn, I don't know what I'm saying. But it wasn't all me, I know that. *You* did take off, K.T. You can't deny that. And you *did* tell Lurlene you thought our relationship was over. Believe me, that came as news to me."

She made a face. "What are you talking about?"

"Julie overheard you in the bathroom."

Footsteps clanged on the steps. A man decked out like an ad for the Gap skipped by us.

K.T. shuffled her feet. "Maybe I did say something like that."

"For God's sake, why?"

This time when our eyes met the electricity stung. Her mouth quivered. "You can't make a commitment, Robin. I knew that then and I know that now. *You* can't make a commitment and *I* desperately want a family. Not a relationship. Not another lover in a never-ending stream of lovers. I want a family." She blinked away tears. "You wouldn't understand."

I wanted to stop her from leaving me, but I couldn't. The door whispered shut behind her. How could I have a family? I doubted we even defined *family* the same way. Family to me was a force to resist, a captivity to escape. Silence, clenched jaws, cries unanswered in the night. A steel splinter under the skin your body patiently and painfully struggles to expel.

And a child? I'd never considered the possibility. You had to be grown-up to have a kid. Selfless. Willing to sacrifice life, limb, libido, not to mention income, independence and any semblance of sanity. But seeing K.T. again felt like undergoing angioplasty. There was no question about it. I was as much in love with her now as I was seven months ago. I had a few options. I could burst into K.T.'s meeting, sweep her into my arms and profess my undying love. Or I could slink away into the dark and get on with my investigation.

In the end, I didn't really have a choice. I was up to my ears in Phyl's life. And then there was

Michael. The last night I spent with him I had taught him to say Yoo-Hoo, or some jumble of sounds that came pretty damn close. In my world, that constituted an irrefutable obligation.

I brushed a hand over the door to the Wilde room, blinked twice, then clanged downstairs. It wasn't until I was behind the wheel again that I realized the full impact of running into K.T. My skin felt as if it were encased in dry ice, hot and cold sensations flashing over me in quick waves. I turned on the ignition when suddenly a high-pitched wail echoed through the car. I slammed through the driver's door and hit the gutter, hands over my head. The shrill whistling grew louder, ringing in my ears and reverberating throughout my body. A taxi splashed by and I sucked in a mouthful of filthy sludge. Five minutes later, the car still had not blown up.

"Hey, lady, you okay?"

I glanced up at an elderly man carrying a soggy loaf of Italian bread. I now define rock-bottom as being helped to your feet by an eighty-year-old guy balancing himself with a cane. As soon as I stood up, understanding sank in. I unzipped my jacket. The damn battery on my beeper had died, causing its alarm to buzz like a banshee. I slipped the old man a ten, as much to alleviate my embarrassment as to buy his silence in case we ever met again and returned to the car. The entire front of my body was soaking wet and black with soot. I reached into my pants, relieved to find the thermals were still dry. I slid out of my jeans, draped them over the glove compartment and aimed the air vents at them.

I plowed through the slush and headed to

Justin's. My luck, traffic was light and I found a parking spot almost immediately. There was no time for the jeans to dry out, but I had no choice. I shimmied into them, grimacing the whole time. The exertion wiped me out. I leaned back and gulped air. I opened the car door, swung my legs out and held onto the window frame. My knees felt like butter slipping over hot corn. If I didn't get some sleep soon, I was going to collapse. I wobbled toward the lobby. The doorman zipped over right away, disgust etched into the scowl on his lips. I could tell in one glance that this guy took his work seriously.

"No handouts here, so move it. Come on, come on." He had me by the elbow and steered me back outside.

I dug my heels in and said, "Call up to Justin Kleinbaum. Tell him Robin Miller's here."

He brushed his hat back from his forehead and took another look at me. His hair reminded me of a tabby's back. "Mr. Kleinbaum's not home."

Of course. He was out of town visiting his father. "Then talk to Matthew."

Genuine surprise flickered across his face. "You know Matt?"

I guessed from his inflection that he considered Matthew's existence privileged information. I said, "Call him."

Five minutes later Matthew ushered me into the living room. I didn't think it was possible for anyone to look worse than me, but he came close. He wore a T-shirt and pajama bottoms. His skin had a gray sheen. He was unshaven and possibly unwashed. I could smell perspiration rising from him. There was a raw spot on his lower lip, where even now his teeth

144

gnawed nervously. Yesterday his eyes had reminded me of chocolate. Tonight they were melting.

We were alone in the apartment. I knew that immediately. Matthew locked the door behind me, then leaned his forehead against the metal, his fingers still clenched around the deadbolt. I turned away from him. Neither of us spoke.

There are some silences that are less the absence of sound than the absence of life. All at once I recalled a class trip to Washington, D.C. At one point on the tour I separated from the group and wound up staring at the bed where Lincoln had died. I gawked at the bloodstained pillow, suddenly deaf to all sound except a strange hiss that seemed to radiate from inside my own head. I closed my eyes tight, believing that if I tried really hard I could hear words whispered in that very room decades before I was born. A similar sensation overtook me now. Neither Justin nor Elana was there, but I felt them all around me.

Plastic building blocks spilled from a beach pail that had tipped on its side. A menagerie of stuffed animals clustered to one side of the crib, which was positioned prominently in front of a bank of windows overlooking the Hudson River. A mission-style coffee table held stacks of blueprints and a Rolodex file. Positioned on top, as if it were a paperweight, was a cordless phone. Justin's slippers peeked out from under the sofa. I wanted to run and flick on a radio or the Weather Channel.

We padded across the Oriental rug and sat on opposite ends of a couch covered with baby-stained sheets. This time when our eyes met I felt startled. There was a grief in Matthew, a yearning loneliness,

I had not witnessed in Phyllis. This man missed his family desperately. What unsettled me most, though, was my response. Something in me vibrated with him.

"Where's Elana?" I asked at last.

"Justin dropped her off at his cousin's house. He didn't think I was up to child-care right now." He plucked on an eyebrow and said, "I gather there's been no news. Doesn't mean anything, though, right? Why would there be more contact? The terms are set. Now it's just a financial transaction." He broke off, pressed his index finger and thumb against his eye sockets. He sniffed and pitched me a wan smile.

"I went to the Center tonight."

"I wasn't there. I didn't make it into work either. When I woke up this morning, I had this incredible moment of peace. Justin was curled around me, his arm around my belly. I could hear Elana muttering to herself over the room monitor. We had the blinds up and the sky was simply magnificent. Salmon pink and lilac. And then it hit me. My son could be dead." His voice cracked.

I waited for him to continue. He reached out suddenly and grasped my hand. I squeezed back.

"I've never been so scared," he whispered.

"When's Justin due back?"

He shook his head. "An hour or so. It might as well be forever. He offered to stay behind but I was stupid enough to slip into some macho, me-big-boy-now mode. I practically shoved him out the door, but as soon as it shut behind him, I fell apart. God, I want my family back. I didn't know it was possible to feel this much pain and not be on the verge of death." He glanced at our hands, emitted a sound that was half-laugh, half-sob. "Listen to me. Talk about being a wuss." He removed his hand and faced me. "So why are you here?"

For the life of me, I couldn't remember. Matthew transformed the word *family* into a hieroglyphic whose shape, meaning and derivation I could not understand. I flipped open my briefcase, whipped out my notepad and collected myself.

"You wanted custody of Michael." My inflection was flat. His response was anything but.

"Of course I did. He's my son, probably the only child I'll ever father. And when it comes down to it, Michael, or rather the *idea* of Michael, was the only reason I married Phyllis in the first place. I practically badgered her into having a kid. For one thing, it meant having sex, an ordeal both of us avoided at all costs. After the first five years, our relationship became entirely platonic. We kept trying . . . not to have a kid, but just to have sex. My body wouldn't cooperate. We'd get down to the moment of truth and there it'd go. *Whoop.* So we went the turkey baster route. Phyllis got pregnant on the first try. I was ecstatic. She panicked. Suddenly she realized that she had wasted a decade of her life trying to be the good girl Roth. She wanted passion. She wanted sex. Lots of it. She raced into an affair with this female cop so fast I couldn't believe it. There she was, carrying our baby and catting around like a teenager. I didn't see her at all for two months and when I did she told me she was filing for a divorce. That woke me up, all right. I went through my own crazies. Philly got my juices going. I was so naïve. I thought, cool, we'll both come out, raise our kid together as friends. I called up my parents, then hers. Big boo-boo. They totally freaked. Her folks, not mine. My dad said, 'Don't get sick,' and my mom said, 'Get Michael.' I was with her on that count. But the Roths went ballistic. Called me all kinds of names. To be fair, it was Oscar. Harriet's hardly more than a shadow, really. Who knows what she really thinks? Tell you something, I always got the sense she knew exactly what was going on, or not going on, with me and Phyl."

I had a brief coughing fit. Matthew shot me a look of surprise, as if I had just arrived on the scene. He reached out and brushed a palm over my pants.

"You're soaking wet. Come on."

He led me into the bedroom, excavated a set of drawers like a dog digging for a lost bone. When he was done, the floor was littered with a pair of worn jeans, clean socks, two cotton sweaters and a pair of boxer shorts. "Take what you need." He gathered the pile in his arms and dumped it on the bed. "I can't believe I let you sit there like that. Sorry."

I didn't argue with him. Matter of fact, I decided to hustle myself into the shower. I exited fifteen minutes later, a tired lesbian in ill-fitting men's clothes. If only it were the Fifties, I mused. I stopped back in the bedroom briefly, dialed my apartment, then my housemates. Both lines were busy. I prayed that was a positive sign.

Matthew was in the kitchen, spooning honey into a mug of milky tea. "This is an old remedy of my mom's." I listened to the spoon clang noisily against the sides of the mug. He ripped open a bag of anisette toast, shook eight or nine pieces onto a plate and gestured for me to sit. Maybe if things didn't work out between him and Justin, he'd consider marrying me.

The tea went down easy. I detected just a hint of rum. "Why didn't you get custody?"

He fingered crumbs off the plate and brought them to his lips. "You're kidding, right? Phyllis would've given me custody, no problem there. If it were only the two of us, we could've worked up a terrific arrangement. But Oscar Roth would've slit his wrists first. Or mine. He's convinced I'm going to molest Michael. That's what he told Phyl. Of course, she's all squeaky clean in this. What I didn't realize back then was that Phyllis had no intention of coming out of the closet. She just wanted to drag some women in there with her. I begged her to tell the truth, or at least back me up. But Oscar's got strings on her that can't be cut."

"What kind of strings?"

"Honest? Well, the man's worth over twenty mil. Phyllis and Michael are the only heirs. Figure it out for yourself. Not that Phyl is money hungry. She's not. What always impressed me about her was how little she cared for all that stuff. But still, we're talking twenty mil. My folks are worth ten grand. Twenty tops. Taking the high road with them didn't cost me much. Didn't cost me anything."

I watched a piece of anisette toast break off and dissolve in my tea. A question percolated in my gut and the prospect of letting the words rise to my lips made me feel sick. I put down the mug and asked, "Is it possible Phyl's behind this?"

Matthew started. "Whoa! If that's what you think I'm saying, you're way off. Phyllis is no angel, for sure, but she's not capable of . . . crap. I can't even believe you're saying this. I thought you and Phyl —"

"It's not the same as you and Justin." The words spilled out.

"Oh." He played with a cuticle. "Does she know?"

"Hey, I'm conducting this interrogation. Remember?"

He grinned sheepishly. "I forgot."

This guy thrived on company. I couldn't believe how much better he looked now than when I first arrived. I felt guilty for asking the next question. "How well do you know Justin?"

"Very well." The answer was quick, confident rather than defensive. He stood and grabbed a phone off the hook. He punched in some numbers and handed the receiver to me. A woman answered, "Springfield General."

Matthew said, "Ask for an update on Saul Kleinbaum. Say you're his daughter Patty."

I did as he asked. She switched me to a different nursing station. Another woman got on and told me Mr. Kleinbaum was still in recovery but assured me the bypass surgery had gone very well. She added that my brother had left the hospital about two hours ago.

Matthew watched me hang up, his lips pursed smugly. "That's where Justin was today. I know him like I know this hand." He held his right palm out. "He loves Michael as much as he loves me and he wants our family to be complete. We both do. But we're not kidnappers. We're squirreling away every dime we have. We're working with a lawyer from Lambda Legal Defense. It's going to take time, but we'll get Michael." His swagger stumbled and he swallowed hard. "But first, you have to find him. Please."

I knew he could be snowing me, but I wanted to believe him. "Have you had any contact at all with a man named Edison Graves?"

He frowned and shook his head.

"How about Elmore Wilmington?" I described him in great detail. Again he said no.

"Do you know Joyce Gass?"

"Yeah, sure. We're pretty good friends. She's kind of shy and hard to get to know but once you do, she's incredible. Her husband's a lawyer. Russ has been almost as helpful as the people at Lambda."

"I take it she doesn't like Phyllis."

"She thinks she's a hypocrite. And she despises Oscar Roth. But if you're investigating her, you are way off track."

In the bowling alley of my imagination, I removed another pin. "What about Alexander?"

"Karen? I don't know. What does Phyllis say?"

"She trusts her. But I don't. Do you know she closed down Second Home?"

"So? Maybe that's a good sign. Maybe she was too upset to work. Or just worried about the other kids."

"Have you ever met her husband?"

"Tripp? No. I've only heard about him from Phyl." Matthew had stopped making eye contact. He was back to picking at a cuticle with amazing concentration. I took that as a bad sign. For the first time this evening I felt sure he was holding something back.

I said his name. He responded in a little boy

voice, still inspecting his fingernails. I had to play dirty. "How badly do you want to see Michael again?"

A single, guttural sob racked his body. He doubled over, his chin between his knees, hands clasped over his head, a man desperately trying to protect himself from fallout of a life being blown apart. I stroked his back until the shudders ceased. After a minute or two he sat up, shifted away from me. He looked scared. "This is probably nothing, you know. Still, it's been bugging me."

I told him to continue.

"I got this secondhand from Phyllis, months ago. I asked her yesterday how she found out all this crap and she said I was worrying about nothing. She's probably right. She knows Karen a lot better than I do."

"Sometimes familiarity clouds judgment."

He nodded vigorously, as if Buddha had spoken directly to him. "Yeah. Maybe. Well, one time, I think it was early fall, I picked Michael up at the center. I left his diaper bag behind and Karen ran out to the car to call me back. It was the first time I realized how bad her limp was. Have you noticed it? Yeah? Well, I guess I'm not real observant. Anyway, when I dropped Michael off I asked Phyllis about it and she got all melancholy. 'Poor Karen.' That's what she said. I asked her why and she told me that Karen used to be a school teacher. Right here, at P.S. 321. Phyl looked at me strangely about then and cut herself off. I said something like, you're calling her poor Karen because she used to teach? Phyl looked at me like I was an asshole, which was basically how she looked at me for the second half of

152

our marriage, so it didn't stop me. I kept bugging her and finally she agreed to confide in me as long as I promised to keep my mouth shut."

I took a sip of tea and nodded at him to continue.

"Karen and Tripp... that's the husband's nickname, by the way. His full name's Aaron Trippler. Karen and Tripp had been trying to have a kid for five or six years. As soon as I heard that, believe me, I could relate. Anyway, they went for in vitro and she got pregnant on the third try. This was in the mid-Eighties. Three months later, she was viciously raped and beaten in the schoolyard. She lost the baby and had to have a hysterectomy. Phyl and I were living in the neighborhood at the time this happened, so she assumed I'd remember the story right away. Apparently it got a lot of press. Some jerk from the *Post* spilled Karen's name and she started getting all these crank calls. Worst part is the cops never caught the guy. Karen quit her job, became really reclusive and paranoid, even changed her name a couple of times. She wanted to move out of state, but at the time her husband had this big deal job with Brooklyn Union Gas. They compromised on a different neighborhood."

"Do you know when she assumed the name Alexander?"

"No. But I'm not even sure that's her official name. You know, on tax records and shit like that. Phyl makes the checks out to Mrs. Aaron Trippler. But I didn't finish what I was saying."

"Go ahead."

"The day the baby her baby would've been due, Karen jumped out a window of the building they were living in back then. Fifth floor. She shattered her hip bone. This was back in eighty-six, eighty-seven, I think. They've moved since then."

I felt my eyes widen. I've seen women suffer less atrocity and carry more apparent emotional damage. Karen Alexander had always struck me as impervious to suffering or fear. Pioneer woman on the urban frontier. "How'd she end up with a day-care center?"

"Got me. She opened Second Home little over a year ago. Believe me, I wouldn't have let Phyllis send Michael there unless I felt Karen was absolutely capable. I interviewed her myself." He sounded defensive.

I squeezed his shoulder. "What else, Matthew?"

He frowned. "This is all hearsay, you know? God. Phyl's going to slay me for this."

"I'll take care of Phyllis."

"Good luck. Okay. Here goes. Karen and Tripp have been having a really hard time again lately, about the baby issue. All I know is Karen desperately wants a child. That's what Phyl said, exactly. *Desperately.* At one point Karen even asked her if she'd consider being a surrogate mom. You know what I mean?"

I felt my blood quicken. "She wanted Phyllis to get pregnant with her husband's sperm?"

He grimaced at me and nodded. "Phyl refused outright. Then a couple of months ago I overheard her talking to Karen on the phone. Apparently she found a woman who'd go along with the plan. I knew who she was talking about. The woman's a dead ringer for Demi Moore, educated, artistic and disease-free. Only problem, the woman wanted seventy-five grand, plus medical expenses." He took a deep breath. "Karen didn't have the money and Phyl refused to loan it to her. But they didn't give up. According to Phyl, Karen said, 'I'll either find someone cheaper, or I'll find the money. Whatever it takes.' "

Chapter 8

Adrenaline drove me. The roads were slick and the glare of tail lights and street lamps burned my eyes. Despite the pounding in my chest, I managed to keep my pace slow and steady. In the bowels of the Battery Tunnel I choked. The lanes were too damn narrow. Exhaust crept into the car through unseen crevices, and the dim yellow illumination made me woozy. I clutched the steering wheel and leaned forward. When I glanced down at the speedometer, the needle just topped twenty-five.

By the time I pulled up to Karen Alexander's

place, it was almost ten-thirty. I was in Windsor Terrace, a quiet, working-class neighborhood bordering Park Slope. People either lived here their entire adult lives, generation after generation, or moved here from other parts of the city when they got fed up paying top dollar for apartments more appropriately sized for Barbie and Ken than human beings with full-length limbs. I'd wrangled the address out of Matthew after assuring him repeatedly that I had no intention of breaking into Karen's apartment if she wasn't home.

I lied.

Karen lived in one of a row of connected brick-faced homes, each with its own shallow driveway and four-by-four front garden. I'd seen similar structures in Chicago, Boston and even New Orleans. Give a diehard city dweller a square of grass and the poor deluded soul will swear it's the suburbs. I double-parked the car by the corner and then practically skated down the block. The building had two stories. Karen Alexander lived on the top. The lights were out on both floors. No one answered the doorbell. This time, I didn't even bother glancing over my shoulder. With tight-lipped determination, I snapped through the locks on the door leading to the upstairs apartment and stepped inside.

No alarms. No dogs. A thick Blue Spruce blocked the window overlooking the street. I could've popped a bottle of champagne. Instead I blew my nose, then I flicked on a pen flashlight and assessed the layout. The place was furnished modestly. The blue velveteen couch and matching recliner were pure Sears. So was the walnut veneer coffee table. I flipped through the magazines strewn over the top. *Good Housekeeping,*

Mother Jones and several parenting magazines. I smiled grimly.

The wall unit was neatly arranged. One shelf held framed photographs, another assorted knickknacks from tourist spots across the country. I picked up a plaster model of Graceland and thought, this must be her husband's taste. No matter how hard I tried, I couldn't see Karen Alexander as an Elvis groupie. I beamed the light over the photographs. There were several of Karen and her husband. Aaron Trippler had the body of a basketball player — all legs, tight butt. He had a wide nose, with a distinct bump on the ridge. His thick, black hair was wavy and almost shoulder-length and, in the photograph I was examining, wind-blown. I recognized the setting as the Boston Harbor Hotel, one of my favorite retreats. He was leaning back on a wood railing, decked out in hunter-green denim that complemented his striking hazel eyes. His top shirt buttons were open, revealing a smooth, hairless, well-defined chest. The smile he flashed at the camera was model perfect. Great teeth, deep dimples and sexy as hell.

I replaced the photograph and moved on. There was a nice-sized dining room off to the right of a central hall. The kitchen and three bedrooms were in the rear. The first room I entered was small, windowless, no bigger than eight by eight. It held two items: a formica-white crib and changing table. I scrambled inside and took a closer look. Both items appeared used, but apparently not in the recent past. The crib lacked bedding. The drawer under the changing table was empty and coated with dust. A shiver rattled my spine. The walls seemed to tighten around me, as if the room were holding its breath.

I backed out anxiously. I skipped the bedroom and headed straight for the office. The room faced a small, fenced-in yard thick with rhododendrons and fir trees. I flicked on the light. The first thing that struck me was the volume of computer equipment crammed into the room. There were two desktop units, a laptop, a tape drive, two modems, a plain-paper fax and a printer. It didn't take me long to guess that this office had to be Trippler's. I sat down in his desk chair or, to be more accurate, I should say I knelt into an ergonomic contraption that compelled me into praying position. I hit the power switch and waited.

I got some strange signals that warned me I had entered an unknown realm. The monitor read "boot" and teased me with a naked colon. I'm fairly computer literate, but that colon had me stumped. I typed "exit," "stop," "logon," "start," and still nothing happened. That old sweet C prompt was missing in action. I screamed "Help!" on screen, but the computer just flickered at me nastily. Finally inspiration set in. I typed "DOS," and bingo, I was on familiar turf. A few more keystrokes carried me into Windows.

Trippler subscribed to more online services than my agency. I clicked on CompuServe and faltered at the password cue. Most people I know plug their passwords directly into the system settings. After all, who the hell can remember passwords like belch.rainbow or chopper.rudder? The fact that Trippler had bypassed this universal shortcut drove my interest higher. I didn't bother searching the desk in the hope of unearthing his password. As it turned out, I didn't have to.

I closed the password screen, selected the mail function and pulled up Trippler's in-basket. Lucky for me, the guy was smart, economical and a little lax about file maintenance. He had downloaded twenty-one messages to read offline, most of them dating back one to two weeks. I scanned them rapidly. The first four were from business associates from outside Boston. Trippler was a freelance systems analyst/management consultant. From the notes I gathered that Trippler had launched a campaign to warn other consultants that a client of his, OptiMax International, had defaulted on a $20,000 bill. The correspondence made Trippler sound like a white knight. I preferred to withhold judgment.

After reading the next ten letters, I started to lose hope. For Trippler, CompuServe served as both the "water-cooler" chat spot and the cold call. I stopped reading the letters and instead inspected the summary listing. My scan halted abruptly at a note from someone using the handle "SILLYHP." People on CompuServe typically use their real names. Selecting a pseudonym takes time and motivation. I clicked and pulled the copy on screen.

My fever spiked. Beads of sweat trickled down along my temple. I unzipped my parka and continued reading. The message was addressed "Dear Tripp," and conveyed a disturbing familiarity. The author had arranged for a meeting between Trippler and a woman referred to only as "my friend." The meeting had been scheduled for the twenty-third of January, about two weeks ago.

My friend will meet you outside of Hadley Gardens, at five. Don't be late. She's still a

*little skittish about all this, but you charmed
her like I knew you would. But, unfortunately,
not as much as you hoped. She hasn't budged
on the money. Sixty big ones, babe. Maybe it
would be different with a woman who was
already pregnant. I don't know. I guess what
matters is that she's here and willing and that
you'll soon have the necessary resources. And,
yes, natural processes are acceptable. You've
waited long enough. And as you well know, I
would never advise someone to waste time
waiting. Anyway, honey boy, I hope this works
out for the both of us. (Or should I say all of
us?) God knows we deserve a little bit of
happiness. In the meantime, I think we should
play this very cool and quiet. No more eye
winks, okay?*

One sentence snagged my attention: *You'll soon
have the necessary resources.* Where was the sixty
coming from, if not the ransom money? I ran
through the equation and didn't like my answer.
Karen and her husband had motive, means and
opportunity. Then a thrill buzzed through me. If they
had taken Michael, he could be hidden nearby. I tried
to remember if the building had a cellar door. I
stopped my musing abruptly. No. Michael couldn't be
here. They wouldn't be that stupid. But I was getting
closer. I had to be. Glancing at my watch made me
dizzy. How many more hours did Michael have before —
My heart thudded. In the distance I heard a
distant *click*. Shit. Had I locked the door after
entering? I sniffed the air like a hound dog. Without

question, someone had arrived home. By the heavy footfall, I guessed it was Trippler. My attention snapped back to the monitor. There was no time to search the membership directory for "SILLYHP." I snatched up a pen, jotted down the e-mail address on the back of my hand, then flicked the computer off. The footsteps halted too abruptly. I scurried to the wall switch, shut the overhead light and pressed myself behind the door. I cursed all those years of Twinkies and Yoo-Hoos. For once, I wanted to be ironing-board thin. I took a deep breath and listened hard. No whispered conversations. No one rushing toward the office. So far, so good. But then it struck me. No lights had been switched on. Ghostly illumination from nearby streetlights coated the room, bathing it in a strange twilight.

My fingers trembled and my knees felt as if they had the consistency of raw meat. Sweat ran down my back and between my breasts in warm rivulets. I could've been in New Orleans at the height of summer, garbed in one-hundred-percent wool, and still not have felt as overheated. If I didn't cool down fast, I'd pass out. I slipped my arms out from my parka. The damn thing was bulky, jammed with pure goose down. There was no way I could ball it up and toss it into the corner. I bundled it against my stomach, my breath growing ragged and wheezy. The footsteps were too measured. Someone was moving through each room of the apartment slowly, calculatedly. I started to slump and shook my head to keep myself alert.

Another sound, this time on the other side of the door. There was a curious silence, as if I had just gone deaf. My gut told me I'd been tagged. Blood pounded in my ears and my chest seemed to cave in on my lungs. My teeth jammed tight to still the hissing of my breath, I tried to suck in air through my nostrils. Stupid, stupid idea. Tears sprang to my eyes as I fought the sudden urge to sneeze. I blinked them away. Almost immediately the footsteps retreated, but this time at a distinctly faster clip. I could hear a drawer scratch open in the adjoining room, objects thudding to the floor. My eyebrows bunched in puzzlement. Maybe my assumption was wrong. Maybe my stalker wasn't Aaron Trippler. Maybe it was a burglar. Confusion cleared the instant I heard that metallic rattle and clank.

A gun was being loaded.

I was on foreign turf and trapped in a room with one exit. I needed a better blind. I slipped out from behind the door and dropped into a crouch. A mobile fax/supply stand was just a few feet away. I scrambled in that direction. At the very least, I could use it as a battering ram. I braced my palms against the top shelf, ready to quarterback it across the room. Then that cartoon-bulb went on over my head. The fact that this was not my home turf could work in my favor. I felt around on the stand and found three rolls of calculator paper, a heavy plastic barrel of toner and an extension cord. I scurried toward the entry, one ear keyed to the sounds in the next room. When the apartment grew silent again I knew I was out of time. Huddled back behind the stand, I struggled to keep my breathing even. I needed to awake the startle instinct in Trippler, force him to rush me. It was my only way out.

I counted to three, took aim, then hurled the toner through the back window and ducked. As the

163

glass shattered, Trippler hurtled into the room and immediately tripped over the extension chord I had strung across the entry. He tried to regain his footing, then stumbled again over the three rolls of calculator paper. The minute he went down, I ˙dove on top and dug my palms against his Adam's apple. Except there was no Adam's apple. I was straddling Karen Alexander and she had a gun pointed at my head.

In the instant of mutual shock, I dodged the gun barrel rushing for my temple and squeezed her trachea until she choked, then I sliced her forearm with a strength that rose from some dark pit inside me. The sickening crack echoed through the room. We both dove for the gun, but I was faster and had full use of all limbs. When I spun toward her, the Smith and Wesson strangely comfortable between my damp palms, Karen was stooped over, cradling her right arm and moaning.

"Straighten up!" I ordered her.

She raised her eyes toward me. "I can't, you asshole. You broke my goddamn arm."

Fury ripped through me. I glanced at my index finger with surprise and shame. It was tight on the trigger. For the first time since I'd accidentally killed my sister, I held a gun in my hand without fear. More startling, I *wanted* to use it.

"Where's Michael?" I demanded.

"How the hell would I know?" She remained bent over, rocking back and forth like a rabbi in prayer. I heard her curse under her breath.

I approached slowly. My adrenaline rush was ebbing fast and, in its wake, fatigue flooded over me. I aimed the gun sight at her head, felt my heart kick against my chest and asked, "Where's the sixty grand coming from?"

She flashed me a deer-in-the-headlight look. "What sixty grand?"

I flipped on the overhead light so that I could get a better look at her expression. "I know about the baby arrangements, Karen."

Her eyes widened. "Oh God," she whispered. She raised her left hand and squeezed the bridge of her nose. The other arm hung limp at her side. She didn't look dangerous at the moment, but I wasn't about to let my guard down. I lowered myself into the desk chair and waited for her to speak. "What baby arrangements?" Her tone was flat. I played along and repeated everything I had learned from Matthew. I saved the best for last, paraphrasing the contents of the CompuServe e-mail.

"You don't know shit," she blurted.

"I know that you and your husband are desperate. And I know about your suicide attempt. I'm willing to bet that if you were desperate enough to try to kill yourself, you might be desperate enough to kidnap a child. Besides, the sixty grand ain't coming from a lucky lottery ticket."

"You're so smug." She snarled at me. "Matthew doesn't know what he's talking about. Maybe you should check your sources better before flapping your mouth."

I waved the gun. "You went for this pretty damn fast."

She had to be in pain, but the only evidence was the way the corners of her lips curled down as she struggled to her feet. "You broke into my house. That's reason enough. I promised myself a long time ago that I'd never let anyone hurt me or violate me again. Ever. You could've been an eighty-year-old cripple and I would've done the same thing. This is my home, my space and you don't belong here. Period."

I extended the gun toward her. "For the last time, where's Michael?"

She lifted her chin. "For the last time, fuck yourself."

Karen wasn't ready to break and I was afraid I might be. I lowered the gun and said, "Put your hands flat on the desk. If you so much as sneeze, I'll take you out."

The motion made her yelp in pain. I ignored her, lifted the phone receiver and dialed my apartment. No one answered. Maybe Tony was downstairs with Beth and Dinah. I tried their number. The phone was snatched up on the other end immediately. My partner's not the type to panic, but his voice was an octave higher than usual and his questions rapid-fire. I knew something was wrong at once. "Give it to me straight, Tony."

Karen muttered his name with disdain.

I gave her a warning look and waited for him to respond. He sucked in his breath and said, "It's Beth. She's missing."

"What do you mean, *missing?*" I pointed the gun at Karen and hissed, "Where's your husband?"

Her head sagged. I tapped her shoulder. The expression she shot at me was confused. Meanwhile Tony was shouting in my ear. "Whose husband? Where are you?"

I countered with my own question. "How can Beth be missing? She's with Dinah and Phyllis."

"Dinah forgot to pack the diapers, so Beth went back to the house to get some. This was around seven o'clock. Phyl and Dinah waited at the restaurant about forty minutes. When she didn't show, they got nervous and came home. She's not here. The diapers were still in Carol's room, so apparently she never even made it inside." He paused, waiting for my brain to catch up with his words.

"You think the kidnapper's got her."

I heard him whisper to someone on the other end, then he said, "You left home around seven yourself. By then the note had been planted. But you didn't find it taped to the door, right? And you didn't find it in the alcove, which you would have if someone had slipped the note *under* the door. So tell me this, would you leave a note like that flat on the stoop, with a good steady snow coming down?" Again, he hesitated. "There's only one explanation, Rob. Someone must've interrupted him . . . and I'm afraid we both know who that was."

I found myself tearing at a cuticle with my teeth. A streak of blood ran down my finger. "God, Tony, if you're right, Beth and Michael may not make it through the night."

He lowered his voice. "It's time to call in the cops."

I nodded to myself, then my attention switched back to Karen. She hadn't uttered a word the entire time I was on the phone. I had the sense she was deep in thought, probably conjuring up more lies. Maybe Tony could get to her. "Wait until I get there. I'm bringing in Karen Alexander. I'll explain later."

I threw the phone down and stabbed the gun into

Karen's side. "He's got Beth now and I'm losing patience. All in all, I'd say this would be a good time for you to start 'fessing up."

"Aaron's out of town. I told you that yesterday." She brushed aside the gun. "Read my lips. Aaron. Is. Out. Of. Town."

"Where's he staying?"

"Somewhere in Boston. We're not on the best terms right now."

I grabbed her injured arm and tears rushed to her eyes. "God help you if you're lying," I growled at her.

I pushed her back through the apartment and led her to my parked car. I ripped the parking ticket from under the windshield wiper and shoved Karen into the driver's seat. She drove with one hand on the seat and one on the wheel. Lucky for me, she was a damn competent driver. We pulled up to my brownstone ten minutes later.

Tony was outside, waiting for us. I rolled down my window. "You got handcuffs on you?"

He slipped me a big, ugly cop smile that made me want to cry out with relief. I watched him step around to the driver's side and extract Karen with an unself-conscious efficiency. I didn't stay around to watch.

Dinah was pacing the length of the living room. Phyllis was nestled into the corner of the love seat, hugging herself tightly and shaking her head in mute disbelief. I dropped down next to her. "You okay?"

"This was not supposed to happen," she said in a harsh voice I didn't recognize. "None of this makes sense."

I tried to take her hand, but she shrugged me off. "No. No. Don't touch me."

"Okay, Phyl, okay."

She stared past me. Her eyes locked on Dinah's back, followed her up and down the room. "She can't handle this, you know." Phyl blinked, ran a hand over her mouth. "You'd think a therapist —"

Dinah overheard her and snapped, "Oh yeah, kind of like physician heal thyself, right, Phyl? What about you, Robin? You have any pearls of wisdom to share with me, huh? This is *my* partner we're talking about. My wife! Because of you —" She pointed at Phyllis. "This damn kidnapping wasn't handed over to the real professionals. And because of you —" This time her finger sliced toward me. "Because of you, Beth's going to get killed. You both make me sick." She grabbed her coat. "I'm going to look for Beth myself." She stormed out of the room.

I stood to follow, but Phyllis grabbed me by my shirt. "I need you here."

"Where's Carol?"

"Asleep inside. Dinah just checked on her a few minutes ago. Please, sit down." She patted the space next to her. "I could use a hug."

I started to sit just as Tony entered with Karen. She looked a hell of a lot less sanguine than she had just a few minutes ago. Tony cleared his throat. "She wants to call the police. She says you broke into her apartment. Is that right?" He narrowed his eyes.

"Absolutely not. That's illegal. There's no way I'd risk my license by doing something stupid like that."

"Yeah," he said. "That's what I thought. Now tell me what's going on."

169

I ran through the night's events. As I spoke, I felt Phyllis withdraw further into herself. She and Alexander exchanged a look. The venom in Karen's expression unnerved me. How had I missed the animosity before?

"Tell you what," Tony said. "I'll chat with our friend here while you check up on that CompuServe number. We'll give it another hour, tops. If we don't have a solid break by then, it's nine-one-one."

Phyllis shot out of her seat. "We are not calling in the police!"

"Tell them why," Karen said.

"Goddamn it. Because of Michael." Phyllis was practically wailing. The last two days had taken their toll on her. Her skin was pasty, her lips chapped and her eyes looked sunken. She stood in front of Tony with her fists clenched.

"*Because of Michael*." Karen aped her. "And you're the one God gave a child to. No wonder I stopped believing." She turned to Tony. "Look, I have to get to a hospital."

"No, you don't. The arm ain't broke. You have a bone bruise, that's all. Now sit down, sister, before I bite you." Tony shot me a sly look. The man has a sick sense of humor.

I flipped him a warning finger, then headed toward my office. Phyllis stopped me. "Why is this necessary? My father's accountant is delivering the cash tomorrow afternoon. If we just wait until Saturday —"

"If we wait until Saturday, both of them will be dead. Don't you get it? This is not a made-for-television movie. The kidnapping's real. Money or no money, the odds are Beth and Michael won't make it through another twenty-four hours. It's time to stop bullshitting ourselves."

Phyllis was wild-eyed. She clung to my arm, desperation etched into the lines around her mouth. "Please. You promised me. No cops. No FBI. You and Tony can handle this on your own. I know you can."

I cupped my hands around her cheeks and said her name quietly. She turned away with a brusque sweep of her arms. Her focus seemed to lock on the mirror that hung alongside the china cabinet. She winced at what she found there. I wrapped my arms around her and stared over her shoulder. She seemed so small in my arms. I tightened my hold and then I saw it — saw the fear in her eyes. Almost at the same time, I caught the reflection of her necklace. Even now, I'd swear that the lights dimmed. Or maybe blood just stopped pumping to my brain. I loosened my hold and stepped back.

Spell it backwards and Phyllis is Sillyhp.

Our gazes met in the mirror. Comprehension burned in her eyes. She didn't bother turning around.

"Shit." The word slipped to my lips.

Karen stepped toward me. "So you finally got it."

I could feel my jaw dropping as I turned to face her. "You knew?"

"Only when you told me about the CompuServe message. I am *not* involved in this. I swear to God, I'm not involved. I wouldn't use a child this way."

Tony sputtered. "What the fuck is going on here, huh?"

"Tell him, Phyllis." Anger made my heart beat faster.

"Robin . . ." Her tone was pleading. She raised her hands toward me, but I just shook my head in disgust.

"Somebody, tell me," Tony said.

Karen answered first. "Phyllis is the one that sent that e-mail message to my husband. I knew they corresponded on CompuServe sometimes, but Aaron said it was about a real estate deal for one of his clients in Boston. What a crock of shit he sold me. But I get it now, though. I'd have to be brain-dead not to get it. Right, Phyllis?"

Now I was confused.

Tony squinted at Phyllis as if he had suddenly gone half-blind. His jaw muscles started to hop and I rushed toward him. I grabbed him by the elbow as he began flinging a string of curses that struck Phyllis like pellets of spit. With each one, her eyes fluttered and facial muscles twitched.

"Calm down, Tony. Please."

He stared at me without comprehension. "Her own kid?"

I spoke quietly. "Take the cuffs off Karen, okay?"

He nodded and shoved his hand into a back pocket. I couldn't bring myself to move closer to Phyl. From across the room, I said, "Tell us where they are."

Phyllis raised open palms. "I don't know."

Tony snapped the cuffs off and flung them across the room, narrowly missing Phyllis. She scrambled backwards and started blathering. "Okay, okay. Aaron and I did plot the kidnapping together. Big deal. I know him and I know he wouldn't hurt Michael. The only person who has anything to lose here is my father, the great Oscar Roth, and what's a quarter-million to him?"

My temples pounded as she spoke. All I could think of was, I had slept with this woman. I had made love to her. My mouth tasted sour. She continued rambling, a coarse thread of excuses and rationalizations.

Tony snorted and moved into the kitchen. I heard him emptying ice trays into a towel. A few minutes later he reentered and wrapped Karen's arm. She looked at him with astonishment. That's the nice part about being a brute. The smallest tenderness can make you seem like a saint.

Karen said, "Thank you," and then cut Phyllis's testimony short. "But you're not telling them the best part, are you? I think Robin will be especially interested in the missing pieces."

I didn't like the way Phyllis shriveled up. She flashed me a look of excessive apology that made my intestines knot. I decided to sit down before she continued.

To Karen, she said, "Did Aaron ever tell you?"

"No. I just figured it out from the half-truths your ex handed over to Robin. And from the e-mail message." Karen held the towel in place and sat down at the foot of the china cabinet. Tony was the only one who remained standing.

"I had an affair with Aaron last year," Phyllis said to me. "Before we met. It was amazingly brief." She spoke so low I wanted to pretend that I hadn't heard her. But my eyes must have given it away.

Everyone in the room slid me glances ripe with pity. I closed my eyes and grappled with the impact of her words.

Karen muttered, "And you were the one person I never suspected. Jesus!"

"At some point," Phyllis said, her voice growing stronger, "I started to think that maybe I had made a mistake about being gay. Maybe Matthew just wasn't the right man for me. And God knows, I sure wasn't having a lot of success seducing lesbians."

"But Aaron was easy, huh?" Karen interjected.

So was I, I mused bitterly. So was I.

"It's not how you think," Phyllis said. "He had his own agenda. The third time we slept together, he asked me if he could skip the condom. I said absolutely not, especially since I'd just finished my period and I knew it was prime time for pregnancy. He said, 'Great.' That's when he made his proposal. He wanted me to carry his kid for the two of you. I thought, this guy's ready for the loony bin. But he was dead serious. That was the last time we were together . . . like that." All three of us stared at her as she rummaged in her purse for a cigarette. "The sex wasn't great and there was no way I was going to be a surrogate. But we remained friends and I started to really understand Aaron." She lit the cigarette and pointed it at Karen. "He adores you. Really."

Karen harumphed in response.

"Anyway, a few months ago I told the story to an old school chum of mine up in Amherst. I couldn't believe her reaction. She said she'd be glad to help out. 'Tell them it'll cost seventy-five grand.' I conveyed the message to Aaron. I'd never seen him so happy."

"I think she's telling the truth," Karen said reluctantly. "Aaron omitted the, uh, let's say, *details*, but he did tell me that Phyllis had identified a potential surrogate mom. I was thrilled until I heard the price tag. There was no way we could afford her. I told him that we should forget about surrogacy and adopt, there's so many kids who need parents, but he said that just wasn't an option for him. The kid had to be his, blood and soul."

"Exactly," Phyl said with enthusiasm, as if suddenly her plan made sense to all of us. "You got really depressed after that and Aaron was terrified you'd try to kill yourself again. Then one day Aaron and I were having coffee in Zulu Café —"

"That place just opened in November," Karen blurted.

"December," Phyllis corrected. "The TV was tuned to News New York and a report came on about the Breen kidnapping. I made some comment about how a hundred grand would be peanuts for my parents. And then Aaron and I started playing with the idea, like it was a big joke. 'Okay,' I said. 'You take Michael to Disneyland for a few days and I'll cry kidnap, my father will cough up the big bucks, we'll split the ransom and live happily ever after. Amen.' Aaron laughed till tears came to his eyes. I'm not sure when we got serious about it." She pressed a hand to her stomach as if she felt sick. Her focus turned back to me. "I do know. It was after I met Robin. That's when it turned serious."

Oh, great, lay this crap at my feet. I thought *no*

way, baby. I'm not taking on this one. "Why'd you need money?"

Phyllis looked wounded by the question. She said, "Freedom," as if the word explained everything.

I clenched my fists. "Freedom from what?"

"From my family. And to be honest, in part from Michael. I figured if I had enough money, money that was purely mine, I could finally stop worrying about my folks. Matt would love to take care of Michael on a full-time basis, but can I do that now? No way. My father would cut me off in a hot minute if I ever relinquished custody. And if he knew I was gay? Forget it. My life would be a living hell. None of you know what it's like to come from money, how it feels to have purse strings snagged around your ankles. You can't move without thinking, what if this direction snaps the strings. It's not like I'm Miss Materialistic. I'm not . . . but let's face facts. If I stay daddy's good girl, the payoff is in the millions. Tell me how many people could turn their backs on that kind of money. All I wanted was a modest nest egg, that's all."

I gawked at her with undisguised disgust.

Tony stepped in with his usual finesse. "Lucky for me, my dad died with creditors barking at his heels. And Mom's greatest asset is Medicare. So if you'll excuse my French, shut the fuck up. Now skip to the good part. Where's your son?"

"In Amherst. Aaron's staying with my friend, Gari. She's the surrogate. I introduced them back in December and they really hit it off. That's when Gari said she'd settle for sixty. Aaron tried to get it down to fifty, but she held fast."

Karen let out a little moan. It wasn't hard to figure out why.

I snatched up the phone and said, "Call him."

Phyllis shook her head and flipped ash into her palm. "I can't. The phone's disconnected."

Tony and I said, "What?" at the same time.

"I know he's still there. Gari called me this morning from a pay phone and told me how she asked him to check into a motel and he flat out refused. By the way, she thinks he's babysitting for me."

"Gari doesn't know what's going on?" I asked.

"No. I didn't want to involve her."

"You didn't want to involve her, so you sent Aaron to her place. Is that what you're saying?" My patience was wafer-thin.

"No, goddamn it. I didn't. That's my point. He was supposed to stay at a hotel in Boston. Something's gone wrong. First, he called me at Second Home. That wasn't the original plan either, but I went along. I thought he was improvising, you know, to keep my reactions more credible. Then he turns up at Gari's and ups the ransom. He said he wanted all of the money, not some. I laughed and told him he was getting carried away, but he insisted. The last thing he said was, 'This is no longer a game, Phyl. We play by my rules now.' To tell the truth, I'm not sure he wasn't just acting the part. He acted in college, didn't he, Karen?"

"Oh, he's an actor all right," she responded.

I said, "He can't be in Amherst, not if he's the one that grabbed Beth."

"He's in Amherst," Phyllis repeated with certainty.

Karen chimed in. "Aaron doesn't know Beth, Dinah *or* Carol. That much I do know. The only parents from Second Home he's had extensive contact with are Edison Graves and Phyllis."

Tony and I glanced at each other. Without speaking, I knew we had the same fear.

"Look, wherever Beth is, I'm sure she's safe," Phyllis said hastily. "After all, Aaron's one of the gentlest men I know. He'd never hurt anyone. Right, Karen?"

A strange smile twisted Karen's lips. "I've got some news for you, Phyl. You know that 'suicide' attempt Aaron loves to divulge in those dark, tender moments of intimate communication? Try this on for size. After I had the hysterectomy, Aaron was furious. See, now he was never going to be able to reproduce himself. And he's so damn handsome and intelligent, wouldn't that be a sin?" She rubbed her hip and frowned. "He accused me of dressing too provocatively. Blamed me for getting the *boys* all worked up. It was an old, stupid argument, but that Sunday, it got out of hand. Aaron started smacking me around. Nothing like that had ever happened before, so I was totally unprepared. We were standing by the window and I shouted something mean at him. 'Thank God, I'll never have your damn baby,' or something stupid like that. I don't remember if he socked me or pushed me. All I know is I smashed through that window and plunged to the ground.

178

Next time I opened my eyes, a doctor's injecting an IV into my arm... and Aaron's whispering in my ear, 'You tried to kill yourself, baby. Okay? Just go along and I promise I'll make it up to you.' At the time I was desperate enough to believe him. I've grown up since then."

Phyllis stammered, "But he said, he said, the two of you —"

"Our marriage had been foundering since the, uh, incident." She snorted. "Listen to me. I mean, the rape. But it didn't really hit the rocks until this Christmas. I don't know, one day I woke up and turned over and there was this man sleeping next to me whom I didn't know. I told him I wanted a divorce. He was stunned and so damned conciliatory. I agreed to give us another few months. Despite his affairs. And by the way, Phyl, you weren't the only one. Despite his affairs, Aaron really is a family man. At least, that's how he thinks of himself. Who knows? Maybe he's crazy enough to think this scheme of his will save our marriage. There's a part of me that would love to believe that. But if I had to give odds, though, I'd say he and this woman are a lot friendlier than Phyl knows. For the past six weeks, he's been shuttling up to Boston constantly, at least that's what he's told me."

The red blotch spreading over Phyllis's cheeks spoke volumes. She seemed to crumble into herself as understanding sank in. Karen's instincts were probably right on the mark. Judging from Aaron's history, his relationship with Gari had probably jumped beyond the boundaries of surrogate mom a long time ago. Phyllis had been another well-played pawn.

Tony exhaled loudly. We all turned to him. He was sitting in an armchair, legs spread apart, his hands clasped and dangling between his knees. "Fuck this," he said and stood abruptly. "I'm going to check up on Edison. See where he's been the last few hours. Okay with you, Miller?"

I nodded and gathered up my parka. "You're right. Enough talk." I fetched the car keys from my coat pocket, crossed the room and punched them into Phyllis's hand. "You're going to drive me up to Amherst. Now. Get up." She started to say my name in a sweet, petulant tone that made my teeth clamp together. I slammed my hands around her forearms and lifted her up. "I don't give a damn about you anymore. Do you understand? Not a damn. But as long as there's a chance that Michael's alive, I'm sticking to you like shit to your shoe. Get it? Now put on your coat, and whatever you do, don't say another word to me, unless it's 'We need gas.' "

I slipped on my parka and felt something hard slap against my hip. I reached into the inside pocket and found Karen Alexander's handgun. The impulse to pull it out and jam it against Phyl's back, the ultimate bargaining stick, was way too strong. I scooped it out and handed it to Tony.

He protested, but I said, "Believe me, Tony, this is not my old shit. I wish it was. Do you understand? I can't have this with me right now." As edgy as I felt, I knew the gun could be an irresistible crutch, an easy answer, a quick and brutal solution. I couldn't afford the option. Or the consequences of failing.

Tony tugged on an eyebrow and nodded. "Your call, partner."

"Can you wait until Dinah gets back?" I asked.

"Sure thing. Meanwhile, I'll make some calls. I think it's time we had more help." He hugged me hard, a gesture so uncharacteristic it scared me. I left the apartment fast.

Our worst fear remained unspoken.

Chapter 9

I curled up on the back seat. Twice, Phyllis tried to cajole me into joining her up front. She engaged her best seductive voice, bouncing a come-hither smirk off the rear-view mirror. How could she think I'd capitulate? Her efforts only made me want to bolt out the car door. Instead I tucked my hands under my armpits and said, "You have no idea what you've done." The blank expression she gave me in response was chilling.

I began trembling nonstop once again. I reached over the front seat and swept the heat to high.

Phyllis moved to catch my hand, but I grunted at her and she took the hint. Given the weather and Phyllis's driving habits, the ride to Amherst would take no less than four hours. Maybe five. It would be a good time to sleep, but my mind wouldn't let up. Aaron Trippler had Michael and he sounded like a man whose hold on reality was slipping fast. "Does Aaron own a second gun?" I asked Phyllis.

"So you're talking to me again?" She spoke to the mirror.

I ducked out of view. "Answer the question."

"How the hell should I know?"

"You slept with him. You plotted a kidnapping with him. I think that's reason enough."

She turned on the radio. Suddenly Patsy Cline crooned into the darkness: "I Go Out Walking."

The words brought K.T. back to mind with hurricane force. Unexpectedly, tears sprang to my eyes. "Hand me my damn cell phone."

Phyllis flipped down the glove compartment and pulled out the cellular phone I had been smart enough to grab before leaving Brooklyn. I dialed and got Dinah on the first ring.

"Any news?" I asked.

"Sure. You probably have two more deaths on your hands. Quite an impressive dance card you're accumulating, Rob."

I stared at the phone. Dinah's mean streak was getting too damn wide for me. For the first time in my life, I wondered if our friendship would survive much longer. "I'll take that as a no. Is Karen still there?"

"Yeah, though I don't know why."

"Put her on."

I heard her holler Karen's name. Footsteps approached the phone. The exchange between the two women was curt. I imagined the two of them squaring off in a boxing ring and was surprised to find myself rooting for Karen's side.

She sighed into the phone. "Is something wrong?"

"I need to know if Aaron has another gun."

"Oh."

"Karen?"

"Aaron has a number of clients in the Diamond District."

"Meaning?"

"He's licensed to carry."

I winced. "Anything else you can tell me?"

"His favorite is a forty-five magnum. He wears it in a shoulder holster. And Robin? He's a good marksman."

"Thanks." The odds had shifted against me again. I started wondering if I'd make it through the night. "Stay with Dinah, will you? She may not realize it, but she can use the company."

"The one who needs the company is Carol. I swear, she senses something's wrong. She's crying nonstop."

"I'll call you as soon as we know something."

"Robin, Aaron's not a mean man, but if he feels cornered, he might be capable of something."

"Understood."

I folded the phone and held it to my cheek. Trippler was armed and dangerous. I was unarmed and feeble. If I were a horse, conventional wisdom would say *take the old mare out to the woods and shoot her*. Yet nothing could stop me from trying to rescue Michael. If I had to throw my body between him and Trippler, I knew I would. The realization came to me with a tremor of relief. And fear.

It was half-past one. I stared at the back of Phyllis's head. She was intent on the road. There was nothing left to say to her. Surprisingly, even the anger had begun to succumb to the great, black void pulsing at my core. The confines of the car pressed in on me. I thought about the last eight months of my life. Not a stellar period, by a long shot. Sometime back in July, I had veered far off track. I wondered if it was too late to find my way back home. I fought the impulse, even as my fingers dialed the number. When her voice came on, gravelly with sleep, my nerves sang.

I said her name and waited.

"Hell's bells, Robin Miller, it's the middle of the night."

"Are you alone?"

"What is this? A porn call? If so, you better practice your breathing technique." K.T. sounded annoyed, but my gut told me she was anything but. In my mind, I pictured the way her eyes twinkled whenever she became amused at my expense.

I repeated my question.

"Of course, I am. Do you think any sane person would've allowed me to continue this conversation with you? Which doesn't say much for me, I guess." She was fully awake now. "How about you? Are you alone?"

Phyllis suddenly spoke up. "Who are you talking to?" I glanced at the rear-view mirror. The expression on her face told me she knew exactly who I had called. I covered the phone and told her to mind her business.

On the other end, I heard K.T. say, "Oh, shit."

"Don't jump to conclusions."

"I can't believe you're calling me with your girlfriend right there. Are you drunk?"

The connection crackled. I waited for it to clear, then said, "Absolutely not. It's a long story. All you need to know for now is that she's not my girlfriend and I'm not drunk. Okay?"

"Maybe I should speak to her."

"And maybe not."

"Why are you calling me, Robin? Didn't we say enough tonight?"

"No." I huddled deep into the corner of the back seat. "I love you, K.T. And I want another chance."

"You *are* drunk."

"Look, if you could just postpone this baby thing for just a short while —"

"Oh boy. The more things change . . . Robin, I am not putting my life on hold for you. And this 'baby thing,' as you so clumsily phrased it, is something you cannot understand. Clearly. So let's cut the torture short."

"Make me understand. I won't lie to you, K.T. I've never thought about having a kid. I'm a lesbian and a private eye. And I've fucked up more relationships than I care to admit. It used to be, I'd look at a baby and all I'd see is my sister's face, the way she looked when that goddamn gun went off in my hand. How could I trust myself with somebody else's life? All of that doesn't exactly add up to mother material —"

"No shit."

"*But. But,* I think I'm changing. I know that

sounds lame, but it's true. Give me a chance, K.T. That's all I'm saying. Give me a chance."

I heard a little ping. "Hold on a second," she said. It sounded like she was moving through her apartment.

"What are you doing?"

"I need to eat something," she said. "I think I'm going to throw up." K.T. has a nervous stomach. Maybe I was breaking through.

I listened to her munch, caught the little click of her jaw caused by a mild case of TMJ and felt ridiculously thrilled by the infinitesimal intimacy. Then the connection started to break up. My intestines kicked. "K.T., you still there?"

"You're fucking unbelievable, Robin," Phyllis said from the front seat.

"Shut up," I blurted.

K.T. said, "Excuse me?"

"Not you."

"Where are you?" she asked abruptly.

"My car. On the way to Amherst. Don't ask."

There was a sudden intake of breath. "Are you in trouble?"

I hesitated. "To tell the truth, I'm not sure."

"Where's Tony?"

"Working."

"Who knows where you are besides me?"

"Tony. And Dinah."

"Not Beth?" K.T. was astute. Her anxiety level seemed to shoot up several notches.

"K.T., just tell me you'll see me when I come home."

"Why should I?"

"You know why. I'm so in love with you, it makes me dizzy. I don't want to run anymore." I took a deep breath, or as deep as the congestion in my chest would allow and said, "I need you." That was a new four-letter word for me: *need*. It had the tang of a dill pickle. Guess it's an acquired taste.

"We'll see," she said, after an eternity of scratchy air time.

"We'll see?"

"Good girl. Now repeat after me, *it's not nice to call people up in the middle of the night and expect them to make life-altering decisions.* Come on. You can do it. *It's not nice —*"

She was playing with me and the game was exhilarating. I complied and, I swear, I heard the smile travel over her lips. "Robin, do me a favor. Make it through the night, okay?"

"Sure, Ms. Bellflower, but only because you asked so nicely."

I hung up and tossed the phone onto the front seat. Then, astoundingly, I fell asleep.

When Phyllis said, "We're here," in her newly acquired zombie voice, I was lying face down in a pool of my own spittle and sweat. I grabbed a tissue from a box of tissues that had been crushed by the sneakered foot of some long-ago back seat passenger. I wiped my mouth, blew my nose three times in rapid succession with little success, then rubbed my hands over my face as if they were a washcloth. An engraved road map had been etched into my skin by the rough fabric covering the seats. My back ached and my right foot was asleep. But I was pretty sure my fever had broken. It's amazing how fast you can learn to appreciate such small gifts.

"Which house is it?" I asked.

Phyllis tugged on the hand brake and pivoted toward me. "I can't believe you called K.T. while I was sitting right here. Do you know how that made me feel?"

"Imagine how you might've felt if I had done what I really wanted to and called nine-one-one. Personally, I think you got lucky. Now, which house is it?"

She shook her head as if I were an impossible child. "The French-blue Victorian with the mauve shutters." All of a sudden, she was Martha Stewart. "You know the money could've made all the difference to us. We could've moved up here, lived a simple life. The money would've been ours. Not mine. Ours."

"I have my own money, thank you."

She hugged the head rest and looked me in the eye. "How much?"

"Enough." I pointed to the house impatiently. "You sure that's the right place."

"Absolutely."

There were two cars in the driveway and another parked directly in front of the house. No other cars were parked on the street. "Are any of those Aaron's?"

"The green Bonneville looks like a rental. It could be his. He has a thing for big cars."

I zipped my parka. "I'm going to check out the place. If I'm not back in twenty minutes, call the police."

"I will not."

I gawked at her.

She made a face back. "Aaron is not a thug. I

don't care what Karen said. I'm sure Michael is perfectly safe and the same with Beth. Actually, I wouldn't be surprised if she just wanted some alone time. Dinah's been awfully bitchy lately. Let me tell you, motherhood's not all it's cracked up to be. So, to get to the point, I will not call the police. The only thing that would accomplish is plunging me and Aaron into hot water we don't deserve. I've lost you, he's lost Karen. I think that's punishment enough. Now go play Dick Tracy."

I took the phone and pocketed it. "Keep the car running."

As soon as I opened the door, a bitter wind whipped around me. Amherst is almost two hundred miles northeast of New York City and a good ten degrees colder. The snow here was at least three inches deep and I still wore my Sauconys. Icy flecks of snow clung to my cuffs. I zipped my parka up to my chin and trudged toward the Taurus. I cupped my hands around my eyes and peered inside. A pair of Ray Bans sat on the passenger seat. Maps spilled out from the side pocket. An empty coffee cup stood on the armrest. I moved around to the other side. Nothing. I made my way up the driveway, crunching through a thin layer of unblemished ice.

All at once, a light beamed across my back. I jumped to one side. Phyllis had exited the car. She stared at me over the roof. I waved her back, but she didn't budge. For all I knew, she could be planning to give me up. Trust was no longer an option. I had to move fast and definitively. Dawn was coming soon and I couldn't afford to squander the element of surprise. I fingered the picks in my pocket nervously. The side door was my best choice for easy entry.

The house appeared to swell as I approached. The gabled roof loomed so far above me my heart sank. In a rambling Victorian of this size, I'd be scurrying blindly, a rat in a deadly maze. How could one person occupy so much space? As soon as the thought hit, I realized the game Phyllis was playing. If her friend Gari was so damn hungry for money that she'd agreed to the surrogacy, she sure as hell wasn't rich enough to afford the upkeep of a six-thousand-square-foot Victorian. The place had to be split into apartments. I reversed directions and climbed onto the porch. I glanced back at the car and caught a self-satisfied smile flicker across Phyllis's lips. She wanted me to be tagged. If the cops grabbed me on a break-in, my license would be revoked. Any accusation I'd fling against Phyllis would recoil right back. I had to hand it to her. When it came to self-preservation, she was a genius.

I had one commodity on my side and that was time. And it was running out. I scanned the faded stickers that ran alongside a set of four rusted buzzers. Knowing Gari's last name would've helped. I ran my finger down the list. The space next to apartment three was blank. I rubbed the metal plate. The scratch marks felt fresh. For the first time in forty-eight hours I felt hopeful. Maybe Trippler wasn't so smart, after all. The lock snapped and I slipped inside. I planned to wait until my eyes adjusted, then realized there was no light to adjust to. The place was sealed shut. I was in a central hall, with a steep staircase on the left. I fingered my way down the hall. There was one door and another staircase led down to the ground-floor apartment. Gari's place had to be up one flight.

The floorboards squeaked loudly under my feet. I paused and allowed myself a deep, chest-rattling breath. The place smelled like a museum, damp wood and musty carpets. In the apartment below an alarm clock went off. I took the remaining steps two at a time. By the time I was at Gari's door, my limbs were stone-cold. In the next few minutes, I'd know whether Michael was dead or alive. The deadbolt was stubborn. I jammed in the pick and braced my body against the door. My ear was pressed so close I could practically hear the air humming inside the walls. And something else. Something that tackled my breath. A baby crying.

The fourth time worked and I rushed inside. Big mistake. The oak floorboards screeched and the door crashed against the wall, the sickening *crack* echoing through the cavernous living room. I didn't care. Didn't stop. I tore through the apartment, bumping into unseen furniture, racing blindly toward the sound of Michael's cries.

In the back a man shouted, "Get the fuck out of my way," and then I heard a body smash to the floor.

"Aaron, stop." It was a woman's voice and she sounded in pain. I rammed into a second room and stumbled over her body. It was too dark to see her face clearly, but my fingers told me what I needed to know. A deep gash ran across her cheek. Aaron had slapped her with something hard and narrow, like a gun barrel. Her hands instantly sought to cover her nakedness. I yanked a blanket and threw it over her.

She blathered at me, dropping fast off the edge of consciousness. Three words emerged with excruciating clarity. "Running scared. Canada."

Michael's cries escalated. I banged around the bedroom, opening and slamming two closet doors, before finally finding the one that led into another hall. I sprinted through, my ears tracking the clatter at the far end. Suddenly Michael grew silent. The blood vessels in my temples felt ready to burst. I kicked open the next door. I was in some kind of massive storage closet with a steeply angled ceiling and pine plank floors. At one end were stacks of battered cardboard boxes, old bikes, milk crates of magazines and lacy spiderwebs. The narrow part of the room was what intrigued me, though. There was an exercise trampoline rammed up against a cracked eave, creating a tent-like space on the far side. I edged closer, stooping to avoid a series of wood beams. Pale lavender light spilled in from a circular window about five feet above my head. Dawn was breaking. I picked up a tattered umbrella and used the hook to flip back the trampoline. The crib was empty, the pale cotton blanket soiled with blood. The umbrella became a crutch. I leaned over it and felt my stomach heave.

"Don't fucking move!"

Sometimes it's best not to think. I spun around, using the umbrella as a javelin. I speared it toward the voice, astonished to see Aaron Trippler standing there, the gun in one hand and Michael limp in the other. The umbrella stabbed Trippler's right shoulder and I followed its path like a radar. I barreled toward him, grabbed his wrist and bit down until I tasted blood. The gun clattered to the floor. I dove for it, but Aaron was faster. He kicked it across the room and then crashed his foot into my midsection. I went down like a redwood.

By the time I straightened up, he was out of the apartment. I bolted after him. Halfway down the steps, I heard a car door slam. I prayed it wasn't Phyl leaving me behind. The front door flew open. Phyllis stood there, her hair whipping around her cheeks.

"Aaron has Michael!"

I pushed past her. Trippler was already backing out of the driveway. "The keys!" I screamed at Phyllis. "Where are the keys?"

She dangled them at me. I snatched them from her hand and darted toward the car. Phyl jumped in as I hit the gas.

"Goddamn it," she exclaimed. "Slow down."

"Did you see which way he turned?" I shouted at her.

"Left. He went left." She shuddered and clamped her hands around her shoulders. "I called to him, but he didn't stop. I said my name." Disbelief colored each word. Phyllis was not only selfish and immoral. She was dumb.

The roads were empty, so I had no trouble zeroing in on Trippler's headlights. I pressed the gas pedal almost to the floor. The car bucked for an instant before responding. I hit seventy and kept accelerating.

"The roads are icy, for God's sake. Slow down!" Phyllis seized my thigh.

My back tires slid right. I swerved hard and kept my nose pointed at Trippler. We were closing in on him fast. All the time, I was assessing my chances.

The man stood to lose big time, but he hadn't dumped Michael and when he had the chance to dive for the gun, he chose to flee. I watched the speedometer needle approach eighty. My sweet Hubba was all over the road, but I was still gaining on Trippler. He couldn't be doing more than sixty-five.

"What does your friend do in his spare time?" I asked.

"What? You want to have a conversation now?" She braced her hands against the glove compartment and cursed.

"Just answer the damn question. Does he dive, bike, run, gamble, play tiddlywinks?"

"No. On all counts. He likes computers and sex. Okay? Now, will you slow down?"

Trippler was approaching the on-ramp for I-91. If he made it that far, I'd lose him. And Michael. Everything I had seen so far told me Trippler was a coward. I decided to bank on instinct.

"Hold on, Phyl," I said. The pedal hit the floor.

Phyllis folded herself into crash position, hands over head, and started praying in Hebrew. I could've used a little supernatural assistance myself, but her pious supplication pissed me off. I had a strong suspicion that her prayers omitted me *and* her son.

The car fishtailed across the road. I scraped against a grand old oak tree, lost my passenger-side mirror and kept going, the Energizer Rabbit on amphetamines. Trippler sped up and almost at once the car did a three-sixty. The rear fender of the Bonneville smashed into a trailer parked right outside Hadley Motorboats. The Coolidge Memorial Bridge lay just ahead and a skin of ice floated over the asphalt. I eased up, bit the inside of my cheek until I drew blood. I kept waiting for Trippler to tear back onto the road, but his car didn't budge. My heart sank. Maybe the impact was worse than it looked.

I pulled close enough to see Trippler huddled over the steering wheel. I lowered my window and heard the rasping whir of a stalled motor. Trippler's car was out of commission. Score one for the home team. When I got within thirty feet, Trippler burst from the car, Michael slung under one arm like a goddamn football. He darted across the road and ran down the embankment. A man wild with fear could be very, very dangerous. The only thing stopping me from running him over was Michael. The way he carried him, I couldn't tell if he was alive or dead.

I practically spat at Phyllis as I jammed on the brakes. "There's your fucking gentleman." She glanced over the dashboard and clamped a palm over her mouth. Two seconds later, she fainted dead away. I picked up my steering-wheel club, slammed out of the car and slid halfway across Route 9. The sun was over the horizon now, and the air smelled of pine and exhaust fumes. I scrambled down the embankment. Trippler's footsteps were sharply etched in the icy crust covering the ground. I stumbled over the brambles, my chest heaving hard. In a foot race, he had me beat. I found a steep ridge and slid down on my butt. Where the hell was he running? The road was behind us, the Connecticut River ran on our left and there wasn't a house in sight. And then I got it. He was heading for the old train bridge that led into Northampton. I sliced back across the slope and scuttled through a patch of densely knotted forsythia bushes. Trippler was barreling toward the bridge. I slipped to my knees and let myself roll for a few feet. I raised myself onto my elbows, glanced toward the bridge and instantly started to barf.

Trippler stood dead-center of the bridge. He swung Michael upside down, clasped a hand around his head and suspended him on the other side of the railing. With the other, he gestured for me to approach. I took my time getting to my feet. I needed a moment to catch my breath, to think. If Trippler had wanted to dispose of Michael, he would've done so long before this. Michael was his shield, his bargaining chip. I stooped over with a show of exaggerated discomfort and slid the club inside my parka. The only way to win this game was by letting Trippler believe I was already defeated. I limped toward him.

Down below us, the Connecticut River flowed sluggishly, laden with ice floes and twisted branches.

Trippler flared a grim smirk in my direction. He shouted, "Robin Miller, I presume." I didn't care how amused he tried to sound. The guy was terrified. He lived his life behind a computer screen. Real-life danger, the kind you can't wipe away with a flick of a mouse, was new to him. I had to use that fact to my advantage. I wanted him calm and in charge.

"Good guess, Tripp. Sorry we had to meet this way. 'Specially since we have so much in common."

He snickered, but his eyes were dark slits. "You mean Phyl. Yeah, I guess so. Not a bad lay for a lesbo."

"Actually she's a *great* lay for a lesbo." I managed to smile at him without removing my focus from Michael. I stared so hard I imagined that the boy's fingers twitched. I took a deep, icy breath. "What do you want, Aaron?"

"More importantly, what do *you* want?" He handed Michael off to his right hand. A weak wail broke from his small body. Every nerve in my body sparked. I wanted to spring across the few feet separating us and snag Trippler by the throat. If I still had Alexander's gun, I would've put a bullet through his head. The thought brought me back to my senses.

I said, "You know what I want. The kid. What I don't want is more trouble. For you *or* me. I'm not being paid for that." I took a step forward, winced as if in pain and extended my hands.

Trippler scampered backward. "Close enough." He held Michael between us, his fingers pressed lightly around the child's throat. He gave me the once-over. Standing this close to him, I suddenly understood why Phyllis insisted he was benign. The guy looked like an older David Cassidy — tall, but slightly built, with a baby-sweet face and bedroom eyes. He nodded at my legs. "You hurt yourself up there? Looks like you sprained your ankle. Maybe even broke it." He simulated concern. He was pretty good, too. But I was better. A lifetime of subterfuge has its benefits.

I feinted to my left, in a move meant to convey healthy private-eye bravado, then I winced and said, "Shit, yeah, I guess so," as if I had no choice but to admit that Trippler had the diagnostic brilliance of an orthopedic surgeon.

The response satisfied him. "Too bad." He puckered his lips and his eyes twinkled. Control was within reach, or so he thought. I averted my eyes. I couldn't afford a wrong move. Not now.

"Tell you what I'll do for you, Robin. I'll leave

Mikey up on the hill, near the trailer I hit. How's that? You like that arrangement?"

I watched the rise and fall of Michael's back as Trippler again dangled him over the river. He wore a thin, cotton jumpsuit. His skin looked plastic. "What about Beth?"

"Who's Beth?"

Shit. My worst fears were confirmed. I fought back a new wave of terror and said, "I mean Gari. Her name's Gari, right?"

"Oh. Yeah. I'm going to marry her as soon she gets pregnant. I mean, after my divorce. Gari doesn't know about any of this. Do you understand me? She's an incredible woman." Spittle pooled up in one corner of his lips. Just then he loosened his grip and Michael's ankle slipped an inch. Aaron and I lurched toward the railing at the same time. As he pulled Michael back with both hands, the boy's cries intensified.

"How'd you keep him so quiet earlier?" I asked.

"I guess he was asleep." Trippler's tone told me to back off. My gut told me to get the kid to a hospital quick.

I said, "Babies are funny that way," as if I bought his excuse.

Trippler threw me a sideways glance. "You're not a real fan of children, are you? That's what Phyl said."

"I can live without them. I prefer cats. They keep to themselves. Clean up after their own shit."

"I guess that means you wouldn't want to bear my children, huh? A pity. You'd be hell in the sack."

I winked at him. "More than you know. And less

than Phyl knows. To be honest, I don't think I've given her my best." I was struggling to keep my tone level. The less involved I appeared, the less of a threat I'd pose. "So what do I have to do to get you to give up Michael? And forget about sex. I gave at the office."

He chuckled. "Well, in that case, all I want are your car keys. A simple exchange. This kid for your Subaru."

I unzipped my parka and immediately shuddered. The cold was sinking under my skin. "Come and get it."

"One more request. I don't want police knocking on my door. How do I know you won't sic them on me?"

"On what count? Babysitting a kid outside state borders? C'mon. Give me more credit than that, Trippler. I don't need more grief." I whipped out my registration card and waved it at him. "As far as I'm concerned, the car's yours. You'll be doing me a favor. I'm sick of worrying about alternate-side-of-the-street parking."

• "Pretty damn generous of you."

"Not at all. I'll take this up with Phyllis. Her dad's paying me good money to find Michael. And I'm sure she'll be able to cough up a few extra bucks to compensate me for my physical anguish and moral discomfort. Not to mention my discretion. See, Tripp, you're not so unique. Everybody's got a price tag."

He smiled, a real one this time. "Money's remarkable, isn't it?" All at once Trippler was looking at me as if I were an unexpected guest who'd just landed on his own private planet.

"Sure is," I said.

He swung Michael back over the railing and held him up against his chest.

I tensed my legs. Not yet, Miller, I warned myself. Not yet.

Trippler patted the boy's back. "He's a good kid. I'm going to have a brood of my own one day. Me and Gari."

"Well, I'm sure you don't want a boy's death on your head. I hear it's hell on your sperm count."

His cackle sickened me. "You know, Phyl underestimated you. She was sure you wouldn't figure us out."

"I got lucky."

Over the past few minutes, Michael's cries had grown weaker. Suddenly, they ceased altogether. Trippler held him at arm's length and shook him. Great daddy material, I thought. And they say homosexuals aren't fit to be parents. The world's too goddamn sick.

I said, "We better get moving, Trippler, if we're going to keep this transaction nice and friendly."

He tucked Michael under his arm again and said, "Throw me the keys. Quick." The edginess had returned.

No time for silly heroics. I tossed them right into his open palm.

He bounced them in his palm, then said, "Thanks. Michael will be by the trailer. I promise, sweetheart. Now, get down on your knees while I pass by. And don't move until you hear the car horn, or else the deal's off."

I knelt near the railing and tucked my hands inside my parka. The asshole thought he'd charmed me like all the other women in his life. Not in a lifetime. He scurried around me and I pounced like a panther, the steering-wheel club smashing into the back of his knees with the full force of a hundred-and-forty pound dyke with bad PMS. He howled and dropped Michael, then he spun toward me, his eyes wide open and stunned. Before he could react, I slammed the club against the side of his head, the impact reverberating along my arm. The instant the metal hit scalp, the fury in me died.

Trippler wobbled for a moment, then keeled over. I stepped over his body and retrieved Michael. A purple welt rose on his forehead. His full, heart-shaped lips were blue around the edges. I hefted him in my arms and pressed my ear to his chest. He was breathing, but just barely. I eased his feet under my waistband and zipped my coat around him. I could feel his breath rise along my neck, the faint movement of his chest a half-step too slow. There was a split second in which I couldn't distinguish the beat of his heart from my own.

I struggled up the embankment, leaving Trippler behind, blood from his head wound carving crimson channels down a snow bank studded with pine needles and acorns.

I had no regrets.

The sky was turning the color of fresh watermelon. And Michael was alive.

Chapter 10

On the way to the hospital, Phyl and I did some hot and hasty negotiations. I didn't want to get tangled in the legal web any more than she did. I promised to keep myself and all related parties mum about the kidnapping conspiracy. In exchange, she'd take any heat generated by the Amherst caper. The story I constructed was simple: Phyl, Aaron and Michael had been in a car accident on Route 9. While Phyllis attended to her son, her lover (Aaron Trippler, not me) had wandered off. A stranger (also not me) had picked her up and driven her to the hospital. I fed her the lines, one piece of crap after another and she memorized them with alacrity. The woman had an impressive facility for bullshit. In an act of great self-sacrifice, I decided to let Phyl sweat the remaining details, like why there were no bloodstains and no child's seat in Trippler's car and where the hell they were going so fast at five-thirty in the morning. The tricky part would be getting Trippler to agree to the prevarication, assuming that the man was even alive. Despite our creativity, I knew Phyl would soon have a gaggle of cops and social workers nipping at her tender ankles. Her discomfort wouldn't cost me a nanosecond of sleep.

Since I never under-utilize an advantage, I tacked on a few extra conditions. First, I wanted backup on the scene, to keep Phyllis honest and Michael safe. While I floored it toward the emergency room, Phyl called Matthew and Justin, who instantly insisted on taking the first flight up. Then I had the grim satisfaction of witnessing Phyl's call to her father. She told him the truth, the whole truth and nothing but. I grabbed the phone long enough to say, "Matthew gets custody, or your daughter goes to prison." I didn't hang on for his response. I didn't have to.

I parked the car and followed Phyl into the emergency room at a comfortable distance. In New York, triage would've taken three weeks and required arm-wrestling with hospital personnel better suited for stints on *American Gladiators* than *Marcus Welby*. But we were in New England, where basic civility had not been entirely eradicated by the crush of humanity. Michael was immediately enveloped in the arms of a heavyset man with bushy eyebrows and the warmest smile I'd seen in months. He rushed Michael inside. Less than five minutes later, a security guard approached Phyllis. My cue to exit.

I found a coffee shop, downed three cups of black coffee, ordered two more to go, then got behind the wheel. Whatever strength I had was fading fast. My cold had gone south. Breathing required effort. Remaining alert was near to impossible. I punched on the most abusive rock station I could find, pumped the volume to teenage levels and headed home. The deejay screeched hysterically about "hot rock for a hot pocket," referring to the weather prediction for the day. Temperatures were expected to jump fifteen degrees. Already, a fresh melt swished around my tires. I tried to be thankful.

It wasn't until Hartford that I wrestled up the strength to dial home. My answering machine had four clicks, no messages. Not an assuring sign. With a sinking heart, I dialed my housemates. No answer. I pulled onto the slushy shoulder and dialed again, hitting each digit with exaggerated care. Still no response. I zipped back on the highway, switched on my radar detector and sped toward New Haven.

The needle of my speedometer edged toward eighty. Calm down, I warned myself. Most likely, Tony had decided it was safer to move Dinah and Carol. A good decision. A smart decision. It's what I would've done. I spent the next thirty minutes trying to find somebody home — Tony, Jill, even Karen Alexander. Finally, I dialed my apartment again. This time it was busy. I sighed so heavily my chest hurt. I finished my fifth cup of coffee, my blood zinging on caffeine, and hit redial. By the third ring, I knew there'd be no answer. Instead I found three more hangups on my machine. Something was horribly wrong. And I had at least two more hours of travel time ahead of me.

The minutes ticked by. I tried to focus on the facts. Phyllis and Aaron Trippler had devised the kidnapping scheme, a senseless copycat act based on newspaper and television reports of the Breen case. Neither one, I was sure, had been involved with the Breens. And neither one of them had abducted Beth. So we were back with the original kidnapper. Somehow we had tripped his, or her, defense mechanism. Maybe he thought I was investigating the Breen kidnapping. I ran through the suspects we'd already interviewed. Top of the list was Edison Graves. I couldn't rule out his wife either. Then there was Elmore Wilmington. Maybe we had been foolish to eliminate Joyce Gass, Yvette Santana, Olivia Walker or any of the other parents at Second Home as prime suspects. And what about Matthew and Justin? How could I be sure that they were inculpable?

There wasn't time to start from scratch, second-guess myself. I had to trust my instincts, and they were shrieking Graves or Wilmington. I replayed every conversation I'd had with or about either man over the past forty-eight hours. I hadn't been close to nailing either one. But I had to remind myself that a fugitive doesn't have the same sensibility as an innocent man. One well-placed question, one slip of the tongue, would've been way too close for comfort.

Around Stamford, Connecticut, I pulled in for gas and tried my office again. This time Jill picked up. She hammered me with a succession of questions. I rapidly brought her up to date, then I asked, "Any word on Beth?" Maybe Phyllis was right and she had just needed some quiet space, away from Dinah, Carol and me.

Jill's initial silence punctured any vestige of hope. "Sorry. Tony spent most of the night trying to track her down on his own, which was a big mistake. Around five in the morning, I got a phone call from him . . . from Methodist's emergency room."

My first thought was, this is my fault. I shouldn't have gone into work with a flu. Now he's probably got pneumonia because of me. My self-flagellation was interrupted when the gas station attendant banged on my window. I shoved a twenty into his hand, waved him away and asked, "How bad is it?"

"He passed out in his car, near where Edison Graves lives. It could be exhaustion, but because he has AIDS they want to do a bunch of tests. He sounds okay, Robin. Really."

"Where's Dinah and Carol?"

"With John. At his studio."

Jill's husband is a good man. He'd take good care of them. My focus had to remain on finding Beth. "Did Tony actually talk to Graves?"

"Nope. He never showed up last night. The wife was home though. Tony had a little chat with her. I got the impression they may have fought over the little girl. What's her name?"

"Kirsten."

"Yeah, that's it. Anyway, the wife insists that she has no idea where her husband is."

"So what are you up to now?"

"I just got back from the hospital. Tony wants me to see a friend of his, Bobby Simon, a cop at the seven-eight. He talked to the guy late last night, before he collapsed. And he thought you'd want me to get in touch with Isaac McGinn."

Isaac's a local cop and a good friend. I said, "Fine, on both counts, but I want you to leave Phyllis and Trippler out of this."

"Let me assume you have your reasons."

"Custody's going to Matthew. I'm keeping my license. Enough said for now. Just tell our cop buddies that we decided to investigate the Breen case in our relentless search for fame, fortune and justice. They'll read between the lines, but so what? I'm assuming you'll focus on Graves."

"Honestly, Rob, I'm going to let the cops decide how they want to handle this. I hate to admit it, but we all got snookered by your girlfriend. Taking this investigation was the dumbest thing this agency has done."

I started to protest.

"Hey, I'm not blaming you. We all made the same mistake. The point is, we were too close to think straight. I was never crazy about Phyl, but —"

"You weren't? Why didn't you tell me?"

"Since when do you welcome interference in your love life?"

"Since when do you worry about whether your interference is welcome or not?"

"Don't hurt my feelings, I might get nasty. Talking about nasty, how should I handle Karen Alexander?"

"Where is she?"

"Right now, she's home, but only because she's been waiting to hear what happened up in Amherst. Once we give her the go-ahead, she plans on driving out to her weekend place in Amagansett. That's why she closed Second Home. Whenever she gets really stressed out, she runs out to the Island. It's the only place she feels safe. At least, that's what she told Tony last night."

My internal alarm went off. "How's she acting?"

"C'mon, Rob. Think about what she's gone through. She finds out her husband slept with one client, is actively trying to impregnate another woman and is guilty of kidnapping. She's not singing Julie Andrews songs, that's for sure."

An eight-wheeler barreled toward my rear, then the driver jammed on the brakes and blasted the horn at the same time. I turned the ignition and pulled out. The phone line crackled in response. "Tell Alexander what you want, but get the exact address of her place on the Island. And I want her tailed. Right now, my motto's trust no one. At least, not until Beth is home safe and sound."

"Got it. In the meantime, take care of yourself."

Easier said than done. With Beth's life hanging in the balance, rest was a long way off.

I drove by my brownstone around eleven-thirty. The sun was winter-harsh and last night's snow had already turned the color and consistency of day-old Turkish coffee. On street corners, where the sewers choked up, pockmarked sheets of ice spread into the gutter. I found a spot two blocks away and waded home through mounds of slush alternating with salt-caked sidewalks.

No one had shoveled the steps to my brownstone. I stared at the stoop, reluctant to enter my home. The snowfall had been relatively light and I could still pick out the faint indentations made by the wheels of Carol's stroller. I stepped around the imprints and put my key in the door. Since adopting Carol, Beth and Dinah spent more time at home than ever before. I'd grown used to the constant murmur, buzz and whine emanating from their apartment. It was like having one of those white-noise machines, the ones you can set to *ocean waves* or *a summer night, with crickets*, only this one was switched on *family*. The silence was deadly.

I wish I could say my cats rushed to greet me, hero mom home from battle and ready to deliver cuddles and pulverized liver. I called them to no avail. Geeja was curled up on the couch. She half-opened one eye, yawned and returned to her corkscrew slumber. My other girl was missing in action. So much for felines. I momentarily fantasized about running out and adopting a big, lumbering boxer or, better yet, a Great Pyrenees, then I bussed Geeja on the forehead and headed for my answering machine. I had a total of ten phone calls, all but one of them hangups. The exception was K.T. The message was brief, "Call when you get home," but it was enough to make me believe tomorrow might be worth waiting for.

I meandered through my apartment, trying to figure out what to do next, my mind and body ping-ponging between nervous energy and absolute lethargy. Finally, I stripped and flung myself into a shower so hot my skin turned crimson. I had just rubbed shampoo into my hair when the phone rang. I dove through the shower curtain and dashed into my bedroom, trailing a river of water and soap suds. Whoever was on the other end waited until I said hello, then hung up. Okay, I thought. Someone was staking me out.

Let the action begin.

I rinsed off quickly, got dressed, checked the deadbolt on the hall door leading up to the roof, then locked myself back in the apartment. The kidnapper had to be Wilmington or Graves. Karen Alexander was a longshot. If there were other options, I was too exhausted or blindsided to see them. The hardest test for me was to do nothing. But instinct told me that the surest way to identify the kidnapper was to be around when he came for me. And I knew he was coming. The only weapons I had in the house besides steak knives were a hunter's Swiss Army knife and a miniature billy club. I shoved the latter two items in my back pockets.

I walked to the windows, closed the shutters and peeked through the slats. It was midmorning, Friday. A group of teenagers from the local high school was taking turns racing a few feet then sliding over the ice patches near the street corner. One almost fell beneath the wheel of an oncoming car. This was cause for riotous laughter. The joke was lost on me.

All of a sudden my doorbell rang. I whirled around and stared at the door. Who the hell was that? I hoisted the window and stuck my head outside. An unfamiliar elderly woman stood on the steps. She wore the kind of yellow plastic boots you see on crossing guards, and her brittle gray hair was trapped in curlers and a net. Her red wool coat looked ancient and the fake fur collar was partially detached. Hardly a terrifying visage. I yelled down.

She raised her gaze to me and shouted, "Are you Robin Miller?"

"Who wants to know?"

She winced, said, "Damn," and raised a hand to the back of her neck. "Look, honey, I've got arthritis, slipped disks and God knows what else. Come down here and talk to me the old-fashioned civil way."

I scrutinized her for another moment. If this was a disguise, the kidnapper should be working for the CIA. As far as I could tell, the woman was a bonafide Brooklyn senior, loudly griping to herself with the self-possession of someone too old to care what others think.

I unlocked the door and ran down the steps.

As soon as I took a closer look at her, a pang of recognition ran through me. I stepped back in a fleeting panic. Then I realized why the features looked so familiar. She was a neighbor from down the block. I'd seen her camped out on her stoop almost every day of every summer for the past seven years. I just didn't know her name.

"Is there a problem?" I asked, my anxiety rapidly downshifting. She probably needs someone to change the lightbulb in her refrigerator and, lucky me, it was my turn to volunteer.

"Don't get patronizing with me, young girl. I'm doing you a favor. Here, I wrote it down."

She shoved a grocery receipt into my hand. The woman liked frozen foods and microwave popcorn.

"Oy, what are you? An ignoramus? Turn it over." She flipped a hand at me and retreated down the steps with surprising vigor. "And get your phone fixed. At my age, I shouldn't be your messenger. By the way, you could've asked my name, you know, the way neighbors used to. Shirley Bernstein's the name, not that people your age bother remembering the names of *alta cockers* like me."

The note instructed me to be at another building on my block and buzz the garden apartment in twenty minutes. I ran after my neighbor.

"Where'd you get this?" I waved the receipt at her.

"Where do you think? The grocery store. Go to Waldbaum's and you get one of your own." She was tweaking me. Forty years from now, I'd probably be her twin. The prospect terrified me almost as much as the note.

"Who gave you the message?"

"How should I know? I'm watching a nice movie on television, Clark Gable and Carol Lombard are about to kiss and there goes the phone. Some man tells me he can't get a-hold of his cousin, could I go by and give her a message. He told me he'd send me a thank you in the mail. Like I'm gonna hold my breath."

"What did he sound like?"

She said, "What am I? A recording service? Go home already, you're giving me a headache," and shuffled away.

Back inside, I packed an emergency knapsack, grabbed my coat and left a brief message on my office machine. If I disappeared suddenly, it'd be nice if some creature other than my two cats knew about it.

I sprinted down the street, frantically checking

address plates. Whoever was behind this caper was pretty damn familiar with my neighborhood. With less than a minute to spare, I rang the buzzer of a garden apartment belonging to an E. DeMilo. An attractive woman with thick, black hair cut in a stylish bob stepped through the front door and stared at me through a wrought-iron gate. She was around my age and clearly hadn't been expecting me.

"Can I help you?" she asked, as she plucked a pencil from behind her ear.

I flashed the note at her. She frowned, then shot me a perplexed expression. "I don't know anything about this." Her words were rushed. "Obviously, you have the wrong information."

"No one's called here asking for a Robin Miller?"

"Absolutely not." She stepped back into the shadows.

"Any hangups?"

I read her hesitation as a yes.

"How many?"

"Two." Suspicion had escalated to fear.

"When was the last one?"

"A few minutes ago. Why? What's happening?" Her voice was a squeak.

Inside, the phone began to peal. I fished in my pocket and quickly withdrew my wallet. Meanwhile, DeMilo's eyes shot wide open, their focus flickering wildly like an animal slammed into a cage.

"I'm a private eye," I said hurriedly, supporting my words with a flip of my license. "I need to get that call."

A shudder ripped through her. She glanced into her apartment, fingered my wallet and said nothing. I repeated my request as the phone continued to shriek. Each ring made my stomach muscles constrict, my heart pop. I leaned toward the gate and spoke calmly. "You won't be harmed. This isn't about you. I promise. A woman's life may depend on my getting that call. Please."

"I have a cordless," she said numbly.

"Bring it to me."

She scampered inside. I heard the phone's piercing squeal intensify as she raced back toward the front door. She thrust the receiver at me as if it were a dead rat. I eased it through the gate, took a deep breath, turned it on and spoke my name.

"At last, we speak again. I've missed you." The harsh, masculine voice was familiar.

"Where's Beth?" I growled.

"With me . . . I want the money."

Money? My eyebrows pulled together. Who the hell was this? "Let me talk to her."

"Predictable." I winced at a sound that evoked the image of Velcro strips being ripped apart. There was an explosive sob and then one word in Beth's unmistakable voice. She cried out my name and then I heard nothing.

I spun away from DeMilo's open-mouthed gaze. People on the street passed by, oblivious, intent on buying groceries, dropping off bags of laundry, as if life were normal. My eyes filled as I wheezed into the phone. "Are you still there, goddamn it?"

"Yeah."

"What do you want?" I shouted.

"The three-fifty. Your friend's got the dough today, so don't shit me." I heard a metallic clang, then an explosive, "Fuck! Look, you got enough. Put the loot into a laundry bag by four o'clock. Today, bitch." He enunciated *today* as if it were two separate words. "Drop it in the mailbox on Prospect Park West and Thirteenth Street. Make sure the fuckin' string doesn't fall inside. Then tear your ass out of there. I see any cops, your friend's fucked. More ways than one, you got me?"

"I want to hear her voice again, before I deliver. Ten to four."

"No deal."

"Then no money." Buy the bluff, I prayed silently.

"I'm feeling generous. You'll hear from her again, around three-fifteen. No later."

I couldn't let him go, not when I was still so far in the dark. "What about Michael?" I blurted.

"Michael? The kid? Yeah, I got Michael." In the background I heard a whimper. The bastard muffled his voice and barked a word that chilled me to the bone.

"Let me hear his voice."

"Can't do." There was a muted exchange and then he came back on. "The kid's dead. Beth's next unless you pay up." The connection clicked off.

I stood there for a second, stunned and all too ready to mourn. My chances of rescuing Beth were razor-edge slim. I struggled for composure, then passed the phone to DeMilo, who stood huddled in the dark corner of the cold, brick alcove. She gingerly edged back into the light, mascara streaking down her cheeks.

"Thank you," I said, my voice faltering. I imagined too well the terror fermenting in the pit of Beth's stomach and ached for her.

DeMilo asked, "What now?"

It was a good question and one I wanted

desperately to answer. I muttered, "You'll be fine," and wedged my hand through the gate. Human contact can do more magic than most people realize. DeMilo clasped my fingers tentatively at first and then her grip tightened. Almost immediately, the muscles along her jawline relaxed.

"What's your favorite flower?" I asked.

"Irises."

"Irises, okay. Good." I forced a smile. "By five o'clock tonight, I'm coming here with the biggest basket of flowers you've ever seen. Or —" I swallowed hard. "I'll be dead." She tried to pull her hand away, but I held on. "I really need your help. Please."

She gave me an irresolute nod. I took it as assent. I had to. I foisted a pad and pen upon her and recited contact names and numbers for the local precinct house, Methodist Hospital where Tony was laid up and Jill Zimmerman's home and office extension. "These people need to know that I'm going after Elmore Wilmington." And then I gave her his address as well.

As I turned to leave, my heart heavy as a case of bullets, I replayed the word the kidnapper had blurted at Beth. *Bulldagger*. With that one idiosyncratic invective, Wilmington had given himself away. I glanced at my watch. It was already twelve-thirty. There was no way I could meet his demands. The money earmarked for Michael's ransom was already headed back to Oscar Roth's bank. Of course, Wilmington didn't know that. All of his information about Michael's kidnapping must've come from Beth and as far as she knew, we were prepared to pay the ransom free and clear, no strings attached. Wilmington's ignorance would likely keep Beth alive for the next few hours, but I had no illusions about what would happen once four o'clock came and went.

I had no choice but to go after Wilmington myself. It was already after one. I didn't have time to call the police and sit by patiently while some desk clerk tried to track down my friend Isaac McGinn or worse, peck his way through some insane report form in triplicate. I trudged down toward Seventh Avenue, barreled past the shoppers and school kids congregating outside the corner pizza shop and made my way to Wilmington's brownstone. I was stunned to find him sitting outside with his goddamn bongo drums. The man was either completely insane and sociopathic, or simply innocent. Given the circumstances, I wasn't sure which option was worse.

I shouted his name from two houses down. He jerked upright, then waved. I wasn't in the mood for bullshit.

"I want to check out your apartment," I squawked.

"I hope you mean my bedroom," he quipped, smoothing his hair back from his face like a teenage boy on his first date. I felt my stomach sink.

"Give me your keys."

"Aggressive, aren't we?" His face belied the light-hearted tone. Nevertheless, he dropped the keys in my hand. I darted inside. Behind me, Wilmington erupted in a spastic dance. "Mind if I ask what you're looking for?"

I ignored him and cased the joint the way I'd seen my partner do it, turning chairs upside down, yanking out drawers, banging on the back walls of closets. Wilmington cursed at my back. I spun toward him. "Where the fuck is Beth?"

"Beth? Cocksucker! Aw, shit. I don't know a Beth. Who the hell —"

I rammed my finger under his Adam's apple as if it were the barrel of a forty-eight and said, "Don't fuck with me, Wilmington. Beth's my friend and I want her back now!"

His eyes almost rolled back in his head. He jerked away and spit out, "Bulldagger!" One hand slammed into the wall so hard, it broke through the plasterboard. "Fuck. Look, I've been real patient 'till now, but you're way out of line and the more . . . suck dick! Dammit, the more upset I get, the worse . . . Shit!" His whole left side twitched.

I stared at him, refusing to believe the obvious. If it wasn't Wilmington, who the hell had Beth?

"Bulldagger," I said to him, when the fit ceased. "*Bulldagger*. Who the hell else uses that word but you?"

"I don't know. I don't even know where that damn word comes from." He took a deep breath, apparently fighting back against another spasm. "I say that one a lot. I don't know why. There's lots of dykes in this neighborhood —"

I must've made a face, because all of a sudden his eyes lit on me with understanding.

"Aw, shit. You're gay, aren't you? And here I am hitting on you and thinking you're too smug and stuck up to give a guy like me even the smallest sniff test." He actually smiled. "This kind of rejection I can take."

"What about the word? Where'd you hear that?"

"I don't know. Sometimes these sounds don't make any kind of sense. They just appear out of nowhere, kind of a verbal — fuck — combustion. Talking about combustion, why'd you trash my apartment?"

I had to make a decision quick. I gave him a good, long look and then sighed. Wilmington was innocent. I laid out the broad strokes of the case, enough to let him know that my rashness had some merit. When I was done, I backed out of his apartment. He followed me down the steps.

"What'll you do now?" he asked.

"Who the hell knows?" My last shot was Edison Graves, but apparently even his wife didn't know where to find him. I stared down the street, wondering which way to turn. Every direction seemed to slam into a dead end.

"Want a lift home?" Wilmington dangled his keys toward me. "If you don't trust me, I'll even let you drive. This is a peace offering, that's all. And it's only good for the next five minutes. What do you say?"

"Which one's yours?"

He pointed to an ancient Jeep. I liked the way it looked and felt sick and tired of the cold, so I said, "Why the hell not?"

In the car, Wilmington seemed more at ease. He kept his eyes on the road and asked, "How'd this kidnapper know your neighbors so well?"

I shrugged, but he had raised a damn good question, one I couldn't answer. He barreled on, intrigued by the intellectual puzzle. Me, I was thinking about Beth. After a moment, I zoned back in. "What did you just say?" I asked.

"I mean, this guy had to know their addresses *and* phone numbers. And he knew they'd be home midday. Think about it. This is Brooklyn. How many of us even know the name of the person who lives next door, never mind someone on the same block. How'd he pull all that information together so fast?"

I said, "He did his homework, that's for sure," but thought, Wilmington has a point. As far as I knew, the kidnapper had been spooked by my investigation, not knowing I was after an entirely different perp. He'd come by my brownstone last night to warn me off and stumbled onto Beth. No doubt, she assumed he was Michael's kidnapper. I tried to imagine how she might have reacted. Despite her fear, she would've attempted to reason with him, promised him the ransom money, reassured him there was no reason to harm Michael or her since no one cared about retribution, only rescue. Beth was too damn naïve and honest to understand that there's no negotiating with evil. All this took place no earlier than seven o'clock last night, so how had he set his plan into action so fast? Even if he had used the same tactics in the Breen kidnapping, that crime had been premeditated, with time enough for research. And then there was the use of the word *bulldagger*, clearly used to throw me off track. And to implicate Wilmington in the kidnapping. I asked him about Edison Graves and he drew a blank. I pinched the bridge of my nose and cursed. I had less than three hours to find Beth and no leads.

"You know," Wilmington said, as he pulled up to my brownstone, "I'm pretty good at this. Maybe I could help you out. What do you think?"

I grabbed the door latch, said, "I think I've

bothered you enough. Thanks for the lift," and hopped out. I waved him on, but he seemed reluctant to pull away. Great. All I needed was a James Bond wannabe. I turned on my heel and headed toward my steps. The mailman was clanging through my front gate. I nodded at him, curt city-style, said, "Hey Paulie," and circled around his cart. I was halfway up the steps when the cannon went off in my chest. I ran back down and shouted.

Paulie tugged at his pants loops and turned around. "Problem with your mail?" he asked. This guy had been delivering my mail for years. He was a dead ringer for Jackie Gleason, with a drinker's nose and a fuzzy goatee that annoyed the hell out of me. All I knew about him was that he showed up on my doorstep every day around one and never stole my magazines, not even when my friend Carly signed me up for a year of *Playboy* as a joke.

"How familiar are you with the other postal workers in this area?" I asked, my heart thudding along like a race car with a flat tire.

"Some. Why?"

"You know a Lloyd John DiNardo?" DiNardo was the postal worker I had collided with the day Michael was kidnapped.

Paulie wiggled a finger in his right ear. "Damn sinus infection's got my ears all clogged up . . . What do you want to know about Nardy?"

"Has he ever subbed for you on this route?"

"Could be. I was out several months last spring, after my bypass, but if he did the subbing I wasn't around to know it, and I didn't bother asking. I had other things on my mind, like getting the hell out of I.C.U."

"You were out *months*?"

"Guess you didn't miss me much, huh?"

I made some lame apology, kicking myself all the time for allowing routine to blind me. I said, "What do you know about him?"

"Not much. The guy's a bit of a loner. Hot temper, too. You got problems with him, take him up with the postmaster, not me."

That's exactly what I planned to do.

Chapter 11

I ran inside, tried in vain to find my dog-eared phone book, then dashed into my office and slammed a phone directory CD into my computer drive. I jotted down DiNardo's address then rushed out to the car. How had I overlooked the bastard? He had both day-care centers on his route and he had been way too familiar with the Breens' comings and goings. I merged onto Fort Hamilton Parkway, speeding toward Bay Ridge where DiNardo lived. The more I thought about it, the more it made sense, especially if the guy had been casing out Second Home, searching for a second victim. Suddenly Tony and I showed up, burning with purpose, spewing smoke signals DiNardo read as bad omens. He probably assumed we knew way more than we did. And now Beth was going to pay for our mistake.

I braked at a red light, tapping the steering wheel impatiently. "Come on," I muttered to myself. The light turned, I hit the gas and suddenly a small, canary-yellow moving truck spun around the corner, cutting me off. I rammed back on the brakes, slammed into the curb and cursed. I checked out the truck in my rear-view mirror. Written across the back doors were the words, "You got it, we lock it," in blistering red paint. It had New Jersey plates and a broken tail light. I watched it veer across two lanes of traffic and squeal into the Texaco station on the right side. The moron nearly totaled two cars in the rush to beat them to the full-service pump. Just another jerk on the road.

I made the turn and coasted down the block. Something was bugging me. I glanced down at the passenger seat, where I'd put the pad with DiNardo's address. The guy wasn't Albert Einstein, but he had proven to be fairly resourceful. Once he'd contacted me and made the ransom demand, he would have to be stupid to stick around at his place, betting on my inadequacy as a detective. Besides, I had no doubt he planned to dispose of Beth once he made the pick-up and he wouldn't do that in his own home. That must be why he insisted on the callback being made at three-fifteen. He needed time to get back to Brooklyn from wherever he planned to dump Beth. If my friend had ever been at his home, she sure wouldn't be there now. I halted abruptly as the connection clicked.

I did a sharp U-turn and leaned into the wheel. DiNardo had bragged that his brother owned one of the big self-storage places in Jersey. *"You got it, we lock it."* I ran the light and let rubber eat the road. The truck had already left the gas station. I didn't stop to think. He had to be heading for the Verrazano Bridge. I tried to picture the truck. Had there been a name on the back? I barreled toward the bridge, zigzagging between cars, blasting my horn at anyone who didn't get out of my way fast enough. If I kept this up, I'd have cops on my tail in no time. The prospect didn't bother me one bit. A few blocks from the bridge, I caught my first glimpse of the truck. It was a half-mile ahead of me, but the yellow paint was easy to spot. I lost ground on the Verrazano. Wind rattled the windows of my car, and all around me people were moving with caution. I craned my head, snatching brief glances of the truck. He headed for the token lane, which was longer than usual. Thank God for mechanical inefficiencies. I made it to the end of the bridge, slapped six bucks into the tolltaker's hand and tore away from the booths. As soon as my wheels were steady and on dry road, I retrieved my cellular phone and dialed my office. The phone hissed into my ear like an angry goose. I glanced down. The damn battery had burned out.

I was really on my own now, and there was no backing down. Traffic was moderate, making it easy for me to follow DiNardo without getting burned but hard to close the gap between us. I strained to keep an eye on his tail. He was weaving his way toward some kind of hell, his pace quickening as we hit open road. I lost sight of him for almost a full minute. My heart was pounding so wildly, it was like a drumbeat in my ear. Then suddenly I hit a rise and there he was, a good mile ahead, slashing across lanes. I gritted my teeth, streaked onto the shoulder and rammed on the gas. I no longer cared if he saw me. I'd crash into his ass if I had to, anything to stop him from getting away.

He headed for the exit. Car horns blared at him, but he kept on going, accelerating down the ramp. I glanced into my rear-view mirror. My luck, the cops were all chowing down at McDonald's or Bob's Big Boy. I raced down the road after him. We were in the pits of Jersey. On either side of us were fields of neck-high weeds and swampy waters too laden with oil to freeze over. I swerved around a bank of blackened snow, in time to see DiNardo snake onto an unmarked dirt road. Almost immediately he disappeared. I slowed up, rolled down my window and looked outside. The road was rutted, marked by pits filled with rust-colored mud, chunks of ice and a thin film in which oily rainbows swirled. DiNardo's truck was nowhere to be seen.

I crossed my fingers on the steering wheel and edged my way in. On either side, brittle, winter-gold weeds scratched my windows. The air smelled foul, a mixture of gas and decay. I thumped along slowly, my wheels bouncing over rotted tree stumps, rusted beer cans and poisoned rodents. After the first hundred feet, I knew I had made a mistake. DiNardo had lured me into a wasteland. I unzipped my jacket. My whole body felt moist with sweat and my scalp was burning. Where the hell was he?

The wind picked up, howling through the reeds. With it came the strange sound of birds, a frantic flock chirping unseen in the underbrush. I bucked along until I hit a fork in the road. I slammed on the brake and opened the car door. In the distance the truck's engine rumbled ominously. I got back in, made a hard left and felt my wheels protest. A noxious fume started to permeate the car. My throat tingled and my nostril hairs seemed to bristle. I sped up, my wheels slinging mud the color of blood. My windshield wipers smeared the muck until I could no longer see. I stuck my head out the window. Up the road was a series of small buildings constructed of yellow, corrugated metal. We had to be approaching the storage sheds. I depressed the gas pedal. My gears began to grind, but the car didn't budge. I pumped the pedal again and heard the whine of my wheels spinning uselessly in a pit of mud. The car was stuck.

I turned off the car and stepped outside, sinking at once into an oozing puddle of melted snow and wet soil. I sloshed around the car, my sneakers squishing as the earth sucked hungrily at my heels. I couldn't head straight down the road, my approach would be too damn visible. I crunched my way into the sharp-edged reeds, which snapped around my back like a shark's jaws. The damp air cut through the fabric of my parka. I covered my eyes and forged toward the sheds. Harsh wind whipped the weeds against my face and hands. I could feel small trickles of blood running along my cheeks. I heard a car door slam, heard the rasp of DiNardo's breath. He was nearby. I raised my head. Through the weeds, I could barely make out his figure. He wore a black leather jacket and had Beth slung over his shoulder. He glanced back toward where my car had broken down. Even at a distance, I could see him smile.

I resumed my pace, cutting through the weeds at a sharp angle. If I moved fast enough, I could cut him off. My foot kicked into something soft. It squealed and lunged at me. The rat was almost a foot long. I saw his fangs sink into the edge of my parka and, God help me, I screamed. I pirouetted around, ripping down my zipper and finally flinging my coat to the ground. My chest was still heaving when I felt the hands curl around my throat.

"Make a move and I'll break your neck like you was a turkey and I'm a Pilgrim preparing for a Thanksgiving feast."

I tried to nod and instantly began to choke.

"Easy, baby. It's not your time yet." He kicked my parka into the thick brush and pressed his belly into my back. "Move slow."

I struggled to breathe as he pushed me hard toward the sheds, his hands rhythmically stroking and squeezing my neck, cloying aftershave wafting up from his hands. At one point I tried to make a break and he responded instantly by slamming his boot into the back of my knees. I went down flat, my mouth filling with muck, my hands slipping as I searched in vain for solid ground. DiNardo ordered me to stand up. My body heaved violently and I vomited bile and mud. I made it to all fours and then he planted a foot on my spine and spat past me.

"Before you get up, tell me who's delivering the money?"

I needed a lie he'd believe. I didn't know how much information he had about any of us, but I had to make sure I didn't underestimate him. I said, "Beth's girlfriend," and continued digging for anything I could use as a weapon. My fingers found something and I grabbed hold.

"How'd that happen?"

"She didn't trust me to make the drop. She was afraid I'd screw things up. As it is, they all blame me for Michael's death. I came after you myself 'cause I wanted to prove they were wrong."

"They know Michael's dead and they still wanna pay up?"

I said, "Yeah," then stared with shock at the object I had grasped in my palm. It was the hip bone of a child.

DiNardo hauled me up by my collar. "What you got there, baby? Some artifact of my handiwork?" He ripped the bone from me and held it under my nose. "Robin Miller meet Alice Breen."

I couldn't even sob. I raised my gaze and stared into his eyes. They were as cold as stone.

"I didn't intend to kill her. All I wanted was the money and a little bit of revenge. You know what a slime bag Rusty Breen is, huh? You have any idea? My dad worked for ASA Electronics for twenty years. Twenty years. He's eight months away from retirement and here comes Breen, Mr. Primo Hatchet Man, promising to fucking flatten the organization and save the fucking company mega bucks. So my dad's out on his ass, right? Who the hell gives a shit in corporate U.S.A. about one sorry old bastard closing in on his pension. He was old hat, a fucking used car no one wanted, so Breen had him scrapped. Who the hell cares his wife's going blind and they don't have spit for their fucking golden years? Not Breen, that's for shit sure. Even my bro don't come through. I tell him 'Dad needs some help,' and he says, 'Not my problem.' You know what my dad does when he hears that?"

He dug into his waistband and pulled out a gun. He held the barrel against his temple and pretended to pull the trigger. I would've grabbed for it then, but DiNardo's fingers were way too tight around my neck.

"Boom!" The word exploded from his mouth. "Now Dad's gone and Mom's all alone and who the fuck's problem is that? Howie's? No way. Not my big shot brother with his nice little business. No. It's mine. All fucking mine. So one day, there I am, playing Mister Postman and bingo! I seen Breen dropping off his daughter at the center on Sterling. I recognized him from my father's place . . . and I knew right away what I hadda do." He leaned in close. "Here's a surprise for you. I tried snatching the Breen kid once before. From the playground. But one of the fathers from Sterling saw me and threw a shit fit. He slams my head into a tree, see?" He used the gun barrel to sweep back his hair. "I even got a scar. He's banging my head and shouting at me, demanding to know my name and shit and I start telling him how Breen's a fucking bastard who deserves to get hurt and all of a sudden he stops. He goes, 'What did you say?' and I tell him everything, like I just told you. His eyes light up, real crazy-like and he says to me, 'That's Rusty Breen's kid?' like he'd just seen God. So that's how I got me a partner. A smart shithead, too. Only he ain't got no balls. When Breen fucked us over again, throwing us some fucking Monopoly money, Eddie said we had to give the kid back anyway. I said, 'Fuck you,' and popped the kid. I'm no corporate pussy-ass wimp. I call the son-of-a-bitch yesterday to warn him about you and he tells me he's grabbing his spic girlfriend and taking the first flight to Mexico."

So now I knew where Edison Graves fit in. I pressed my hand against my stomach. DiNardo kept babbling, his fingers digging into my neck. We were moving back toward the sheds. I had to get away fast. I shoved my hands into my pockets searching for my army knife and mini club. Then I remembered. After leaving Wilmington, I had transferred both items to my coat.

"You're not listening," he wailed suddenly. "Fuck this." He slammed a fist into my back and shoved me forward.

By the time we broke into a clearing, my pants were soaked through with mud, my skin etched with ribbons of blood and my muscles stuttering from the chill air blowing around us. We stormed toward the front of the building. The first thing I saw was Beth's body. She lay on a concrete path, curled up in a ball, electric tape plastered over her mouth and wrapped around her wrists and ankles. She still wore the clothes she had on yesterday morning and the stench of urine rose from her body. I wanted to run to her, but DiNardo held me back. Finally we got close enough for me to see her eyes. They were open and alert and the pain and fear I saw there brutally articulate. So was the love and that's what made me whirl around like a banshee, kicking and slashing at DiNardo's body.

The gun came up before I could react. I retreated a step. The first shot whizzed by my ear. He waved it at me and said, "The only reason you're still alive is 'cause I got hopes on the money. Three-fifty g's will do me and my mom real good. A nice villa in Sicily maybe. Who knows? I mean, this shit just landed in my lap. I was thinking about another caper, maybe Second Home, maybe the place on Ninth Street. One thing about the Slope, there's lots of people with kids and money. Then you show up and I think, man, this dyke's onto me. I better cool her off. Beth here straightened me out, though." He nudged her with his toe. "No torture, no bullshit like that, she just starts spouting off about the ransom money and some kid named Michael. It's like God dropped this one in my lap, sort of an apology for how things went down for me in the past." He flashed nicotine-stained teeth at me and shook his head. "I can't believe I thought you was trouble. That's the pisser, isn't it?"

Beth shuddered violently. Her blond hair was dirty, the color and texture of coffee grounds. I knelt down despite DiNardo's warning. If I had to die, I'd do it my way. I smoothed her hair and whispered to her. A tear streaked a path along her soot-caked cheek. "Michael's safe," I murmured. She closed her eyes and nodded.

DiNardo grabbed a fistful of hair and yanked back my head. "Time to go inside." He unlocked the door of one shed and flung it open. The metallic clang echoed around us. "Drag her with you."

I turned Beth on her backside as gently as I could, then I cupped my hands around her wrists and pulled. She winced and I slowed my pace. The damp air had caused the edge of the electric tape to furl up. I grabbed the end and began unraveling it as I backed up into the shed. The inside smelled like dead animals and mold. DiNardo slammed the door shut. We were plunged into darkness for an instant, then he switched on a camp lantern.

"Have a seat." He pointed at a velveteen couch with springs ripping through the fabric. "I got a phone call to make," he said. "You see, I know the money was meant for Michael's ransom and I don't have the kid. Now, I wasn't so sure you guys would make good on the payment, especially for this one. But I did a little interview with your friend and I found out Michael's mom is the one with the bucks. And you're her girlfriend. So all of a sudden, I got me some nice odds. All I have to do is beat the other kidnapper to the bucks. And that's what I intend to do." He kept the light on me as he crouched down, pulled a mail pouch out from under the couch and rummaged inside. "Aw, here it is." He stood up, told me to sit down and cross my legs. I knew what was coming so I rapidly unbuttoned my sleeves, tugged on the cuffs of my thermals and loosened my watchband.

I tensed the muscles of my hands as he whipped the tape around my wrists. On the fourth round, the tape ripped off the roll.

"Huh . . . seems you're gonna get a break." The butt of the gun rested on my forehead. He said, "Don't misbehave while I'm gone," and stomped toward the door. The light sliced in. "Scream all you want. The only things that'll hear you are the rats."

The instant his footsteps faded I scrambled toward the door. The damn thing was locked from the outside. I banged my hip against the metal to no avail. I crossed to the couch, bent down, stretched my hands as far apart as they could go and pierced the strip with the edge of a metal spring. In less than a minute my hands were free. I ran to Beth's side and ripped the tape from her mouth, wrists and ankles. Even freed, she couldn't move her limbs. She started to cry at once and I shushed her.

"Come on, honey." I half-carried her to the corner of the shed closest to the door. I sat her down behind a stack of boxes. "Massage your legs, flex your fingers, toes, whatever you can do to get your circulation flowing. The only thing I want you to do is run when I tell you to, okay?"

She nodded.

I made a quick circuit of the shed, then went back to the couch and tugged at the springs. Bracing my foot against the frame for leverage, I tore off one coil. Now I had a weapon. "Beth!" My whisper was coarse, desperate. "I'm shutting the light." When DiNardo stepped in from the outside, he'd be momentarily blinded. And the final game would be set in motion.

I don't know who he planned to call, but I did know there was no one around who would agree to make the payoff. If he somehow got in touch with Phyl —

I heard footsteps approaching. I positioned myself behind the swing of the door and held the coil as if it were a dagger. He shot a bullet through the door, then another. I heard Beth gasp. Meanwhile I kept count. I had taken a good look at his gun. It held six rounds. He'd already used three.

I reached over, grabbed the mail pouch and flung it to the far end of the shed. Sure enough, he shot again, then he shouted, "I'm coming in. First thing that moves gets it in the head." He kicked in the door. It rammed into my toe and bounced off. I bit my tongue and got ready to pounce. "Where the fuck?" His voice gave away his position.

I slammed the door into his back, yelled, "Run!" and scrambled toward him. He still had the gun in his hand. I plunged the coil into his stomach, rolled over his body and darted for the open space. I made it outside in time to see Beth fumble into the weeds. I headed after her when I heard DiNardo shout my name.

By my count he had two bullets left. And he planned to put both in my back. I turned around.

Blood dripped from the wound in his belly, where he had torn out the coil. The gun, though, was steady in his hands. "Got any last words, bitch?"

"Go to hell!"

He took aim. I didn't want his ugly puss to be the last thing I saw. I closed my eyes and conjured up K.T.'s face. The gun exploded. Somewhere in the distance, a gaggle of geese took sudden flight. I opened my eyes. DiNardo had his hands over his chest, his eyes wide open in shock. He fell slowly.

"Fucking Nazi bulldagger!"

I spun around.

Elmore Wilmington stood behind me, a smoking gun in his hand.

Postscript

I rolled onto my left side. A crackling hiss filled my mouth, the sound Rice Crispies makes when milk first hits the bowl. I flopped back on my butt. At the foot of the bed the humidifier buzzed. I raised my head. The damn thing was out of water. I couldn't call Nurse Ratchet to fill it. She and Beth had already fought long and hard over whether hospital policy permitted such liberties. But Beth was a veteran of hospital wars and had won the skirmish hands down.

Small victory. I'd been in a private room at the

hospital for over a week now. Pneumonia. Both lungs. I had four full days of I.V. antibiotics and life got real ugly for a while. My lungs were like sponges squishing with an overdose of dishwashing detergent. I pictured every cell of my body howling for oxygen. I'd be glad to feed them, but my machinery was out of whack. I used the bed rails to hoist myself up, then I swung my legs over the side and paused to catch my breath.

The morning newscaster had promised a gorgeous day. Forty-four degrees, bright sun, no wind. Not that the weather mattered to me. The temperature inside was a steady seventy-five, minimum. At night, I soaked the bed sheets with sweat. During the day, I took turns sipping tea and sucking ice chips. I stared across the room. Metal bars crisscrossed the windows and the panes were fogged over. If I could see through them, I'd be staring at another block of brick and concrete, with opaque windows and caged eyes. I wanted to go home.

If it had been up to Beth, I would've been out of here days ago, but Dinah had quickly nixed her offer of home-care. My old friend and housemate had not forgiven me for endangering Beth's life. Everyone seemed to assume I didn't know how badly my friendship with Dinah had deteriorated. I did. The fact that she never showed up at my hospital bedside spoke volumes. I just didn't want to hear what was being said.

I glanced over at the humidifier again. To fill it, I'd have to lug the tank into the bathroom, flip on the flickering, sulfur-yellow fluorescent, stand there while the anemic faucet portioned out water, drip by drip, and then lug it back. The task was too large. I shoved myself back to bed.

Yesterday Beth told me that she had finally found a home-care attendant she trusted. The guy was available starting tomorrow, so release was in sight.

"Knock, knock."

I smiled at the doorway. Beth's recovery had been downright amazing. She took a mere forty-eight hours off from work and then returned as vigorous and confident as ever. The woman was far more resilient than any of us had imagined. She stood there in her hospital whites, waiting for me to gesture her in.

"Hey, barge right in, hon, the rest of the nurses do. Four in the morning, they're sticking thermometers in my ear, needles in my butt and devising an ingenious assortment of tortures. Tell me, why four in the morning? Can't they wait until I wake up?"

"You seem stronger this morning."

"Why? 'Cause I'm bitching?"

She shot me an indulgent grin. "Your voice sounds stronger and your color's better."

"Get me out of here and I'll do a fandango."

Almost immediately, her eyes darkened. "I'm sorry about that, Rob. You know how I —"

"Don't worry about it."

Beth sat down on the corner of the bed. Her weight increased the tension on the already too-tight sheets. I felt my toes curl. She glanced down at her hands, folded primly in her lap. I didn't have to see her eyes to know tears were coming. Her bottom lip curled and she abruptly turned away from me.

"Things are bad?" I asked.

She bobbed, but didn't look back.

"You guys will work it out. You always do."

"I'm not sure this time, Rob. She's . . . I just don't understand what's going on."

"It's my fault —"

"No. It's not. That's the point. If it hadn't been for you, Michael would be dead. *I'd* be dead. Christ! I'm the one who introduced you to Phyllis, so Dinah could just as well blame me."

"You guys think about counseling?"

She plucked at the blanket absentmindedly. "We're starting next week." Our eyes met. "This is scary stuff."

I reached for her hand, but didn't quite make it. I plopped back against the pillows and blew her a kiss instead. She laughed. "I think I like you this way. Weak and mellow." The hospital page went off in the hallway. Beth heard her name and snapped to attention. "I'll stop in again later."

"Have you checked in on Tony yet?" I knew she had, but I wanted to delay her departure as long as I could.

"First thing this morning. He's doing a lot better."

"Did you find out if Venus DeMilo ever got my flowers?"

"Oh, yeah . . . and her name's Evelyn, for God's sake. Our lovely neighbor received the flowers you asked Jill to send and said, 'Tell Robin thanks, but next time forget the mums.' She's a nice woman. Thinks *you're* crazy, by the way. I liked her instantly. Now, enough chat." She squeezed my hand, rattled the humidifier, said, "I'll get Ellis to take care of this," and scurried away.

As it turned out, Tony had suffered the first of a series of minor strokes. The last one hit two days ago. The doctors say it's not AIDS-related. Instead, they lay the blame squarely on decades of rich chocolate donuts, Big Macs, hot dogs, scrambled eggs and stacks of toast thick with butter. Beth gave me the news while I was tearing into a box of Yodels that Wilmington had smuggled in to me within hours of my admission. She thought her tirade would stop me. Ha! The only way to survive this interminable hospital stay is by indulging in high-caloric contraband. To be honest, though, my pace is off. I still have three-quarters of that original Yodel box tucked in the side table.

I haven't seen Tony yet, but everyone says he's doing fairly well. The left side of his mouth sags and his left hand's weak. Other than that, his faculties are intact. He's incarcerated one floor up from me. I don't know how we got so lucky, but in an age where patients are kicked out of their beds before their stitches are closed, Tony and I seem to be becoming long-term residents. We've already fallen into a routine. Each day we chat on the phone for hours, in between potty runs, chest X-rays and CAT scans. We've blocked out no-call times, though. Mine is four to five, while *Oprah* is on. Tony's private time is reserved for *Sally Jessy Raphael*. Our last call of the day comes at seven, just in time for *Jeopardy*.

Surprisingly, Tony's spirits seem high. To hear him, you'd think stroking out was almost as good as winning a hot game of Bingo. The prospect of dropping dead from an illness not directly related to AIDS has imbued him with an odd ambition. His new mantra is, "Victory in death." Last night, he told me

241

he plans to take up booze and tobacco again. I guess, until now, he's been anticipating a slow, humiliating deterioration. His new goal is a massive, gonna-die-big-time, mother stroke. I swear, it's given him a new will to live. Go figure.

I let out a good, solid wheeze and heaved to one side. The Formica nightstand was cluttered with a gold plastic pitcher — empty, of course — a stack of plastic cups wrapped in more plastic, a box of scratchy tissues and a bottle of Nivea lotion no one ever bothered to rub into my alligator skin. Not even me. I fumbled for the remote. The television set, not much bigger than an Elvis postage stamp, hung from a metal crane that was the color of filing cabinets. I swung the set in front of my nose and clicked on the noon news program. Sure enough, there was Elmore Wilmington in yet another interview. My face cracked into a smile.

When the cops arrived on the scene in New Jersey to find me, Beth and Wilmington huddled near DiNardo's body, they had a posse of news reporters on their tails. My first thought was, the media's going to have a field day with me. I even pictured the headline on the *New York Post:* Famous Romance Writer Turned Dick Nails Breen Kidnappers! Subhead: Hero is a dyke! Instead, I got second billing to Elmore Wilmington.

I turned up the volume.

"So . . . bleep . . . when I saw my partner, Robin —"

A voice off-camera interrupted Wilmington, who was leaning on his old, battered jeep. He nodded vigorously in response to the question. "Yeah, that's right, Robin used to write under the name Laurel Carter. Great books. Anyway, when I saw her talking to that mailman, it all clicked for me. Bleep. I mean, I was on DiNardo's route . . . bleep . . . and it just made sense. The guy had tried to frame me, like just because I got Tourette's, people would think I was nuts. Sure I wanted to . . . bleep . . . get even. But it was more than that. I was worried about my friend. I raced home, got the guy's address, pocketed my gun and headed there right away. I must've arrived a few minutes after Robin. I saw her car make a sharp U-turn, so I decided to follow her. For a while I lost her in Jersey, that swamp area's pretty wild, but I made it there in time and that's what counts."

The interviewer said, "I understand that Edison Graves is still missing. There's some speculation that he and his girlfriend fled to Mexico. Will you and your partner be continuing your investigation?"

His head snapped to the right, then he grinned broadly and gave a five-second sound bite. "Criminals can't hide from us."

The newscaster came back on. Over his shoulder flashed a montage of Wilmington's paintings. A major New York gallery planned to exhibit his work later this month. He finished the segment by saying, "Next on *Nine at Noon*, Tourette's Syndrome, can it happen to you?"

I turned off the set.

The other half of the story never made it to the press. *Nightlife* never ran an episode on how Aaron Trippler had plotted with Phyllis Roth to kidnap her own child and rip off her father for the ransom. Ted Koppel never explained how Trippler had parked outside Second Home the day of Michael's kidnapping, dialed his wife, Karen, on the car phone, pretended to put her on hold, then placed the phone

243

down on the front seat while Tony Bennett crooned on the car radio. No one grilled him, "live at five," on what it felt like to snatch Michael from his crib while his wife paced right outside the door. There were no news flashes on how he'd planned to double-cross Phyllis, take the entire ransom and run away with an unwitting Gari Zapner, the woman who'd agreed to be a surrogate mother and ended up in love with a man who eventually left her bleeding on her bedroom floor.

Instead, the facts of Michael's kidnapping evaporated like a splash of water on a red-hot radiator. My discretion was only partially responsible. The real silencer was Oscar Roth. Within one hour of receiving Phyllis's phone call, he had managed to commandeer a private jet to Amherst, Massachusetts. By the time he arrived, the local cops had sequestered Phyllis in the office of the hospital's chief psychiatrist. Aaron Trippler had already been found, alive but in critical condition. The gentle giant I'd glimpsed in the emergency room had instantly swept Michael into a secured area of the pediatric unit, where he was diagnosed quickly. Michael had a concussion, a broken leg and suffered from exposure and dehydration. The police were on the verge of charging Phyllis with reckless endangerment of a minor, assault-and-battery and assorted criminal actions, all warranted. The charges not the crimes.

But then Oscar Roth stepped in and waved his magic, greenback wand. The police slapped Phyllis on the wrist and advised her, as I had, to surrender custody to her ex-husband. The hospital administration tut-tutted appropriately and wagged their collective index fingers and then reached for their padded blinders.

Curiously enough, I hear that Amherst General will be breaking ground on a new children's wing in less than a year. The Amherst police benevolent fund has received an extraordinarily generous donation from an anonymous patron. Meanwhile, Aaron Trippler is recovering nicely in a suite at the Boston Harbor Hotel, the tab for a three-month stay paid in advance. His girlfriend Gari is looking for a job on the West Coast, and Karen Alexander, vacationing on the Island, has filed for a divorce. The future of Second Home remains uncertain. Trippler has decided not to contest either woman's decision.

Phyllis has called me a few times. I've stopped even pretending to be polite. I just hang up as soon as I hear her voice. Eventually, she'll get it. On the other hand, Matthew, Justin and Elana came by two days ago and we had a great visit. Justin strutted in with a basket of exotic flowers and a fat, mushy Vermont Teddy Bear decked out like Sherlock Holmes. One look at his face, beaming like a teenager who'd just discovered he had one bristly chin hair worth shaving, and I knew I was in for some good news. I wasn't wrong.

When the full madness of Phyllis's antics struck home, Justin took a long, hard look at the road he was on and decided the path wasn't so different from the one Phyllis had barreled down. He realized that he'd had enough of lies and subterfuge. Last Sunday, he sat down with his wife and told her that he was gay and in love with a man. He did the same thing with his parents. To his amazement, no one was shocked. All his wife wanted was a quick and bloodless divorce and an equitable custody arrangement. His parents wanted to know if Matthew was Jewish and if they planned to keep a kosher home. Period. After hearing his mother's response, I wanted to adopt his family. She said, simply, "I'm not saying I understand or that this is what I wished for you. But you're my son, and the real sin would be if your father and I expected you to do anything but what makes you happy. We love you, no matter what."

I imagine Matthew and Justin will hit a few rough pockets down the road. For one, Justin's mom and dad haven't begun to deal with how they'll break the news to their congregation or introduce Matthew at cousin Sadie's bas mitzvah. But the couple is riding high right now, and that seems to be enough for them.

As for me, I was just waiting for my lungs to clear and my life to begin. And for that good, old hospital lunch to arrive. I heard the cart clanging outside my door. I knew what was on the menu, I'd made the selections last night, checking off Jell-O (yuck), boiled chicken (double yuck) and biscuit. I had to say, though, the smells emanating from the hallway today smelled better than the usual freeze-dried and nuked ensemble.

I tugged down the edge of my hospital gown, folded the blankets around my hips expectantly and glanced at the door. K.T. Bellflower was standing there with a tray laden with Fiesta ware. She was in her chef whites and her leaf-green eyes were on high beam. "You think you're ready for this?"

"Why, Ms. Bellflower," I said, mimicking her southern accent. "I believe I am."

And with those words, the tidal wave hit shore.